AF417204

NEXUS NINE
A TRI-GALACTIC TREK NOVEL

MARY E. LOWD

For my mother who sewed Star Trek uniforms, constructed homemade combadges and Borg implants, and painted Trill spots on me for countless Halloweens and conventions throughout my childhood.

CONTENTS

CHAPTER 1
MEETING AN OLD FRIEND

Mazel Rheun watched her old friend, Shep Bataille, from across the command deck of Nexus Nine Base. The calico cat was steeling herself to approach the German Shepherd. Mazel needed to introduce herself, and then she would see the reality in Shep's eyes—the confusion, the lack of recognition. Shep wouldn't know her. In fact, Mazel probably shouldn't think of him as her old friend Shep anymore. Now, he was her commanding officer, Captain Bataille.

A lifetime ago—or maybe only a few months—Mazel had been certain of herself. Himself. She'd been tall, strong, short-furred, and floppy eared. She'd been serious when it was called for and goofy whenever possible. She'd been a captain of her own vessel—his own vessel—in the Tri-Galactic Navy, and she'd come up through the ranks, side by side with Shep. Two dogs, tearing their way through the wild frontiers of the galaxy.

But that had been Shep Bataille and Darius Rheun. Then Darius had died in battle, and the Rheun chip had been passed on to an unremarkable young lieutenant whom Darius had identified in his will. She was Mazel Rheun now—a small calico cat with pale markings who was still figuring herself out. A few months ago, she'd felt right in her own skin. Now she felt short, and her fur was always bothering her, feeling distressingly long and fluffy. It wasn't long. Except in comparison to a Great Dane's. In comparison to Darius'.

And whenever she looked in a mirror now, her calico patches looked lopsided. Sure, she'd always had more of the creamsicle orange on her left side, and a touch of pale ash gray on the right, but that had just been how she looked. Normal. Now she knew what it had felt like to look in a mirror and see a different face. Sometimes, she still expected to see her old face—his face—and was surprised to see her own. Compared to Darius' symmetrical brindling, her calico splotches felt all off kilter. She looked eerie and strange.

A few months ago, Mazel had simply been herself. Now she was herself and Darius, and that meant she was always herself in comparison—in comparison to who she had been before and who she should have been now if Darius hadn't chosen her to receive his Rheun chip. A gift. An amazing gift. But not one she had asked for, and not one she knew how to handle.

The command deck of Nexus Nine Base was built in concentric rings with the inner rings higher than the outer ones. Between each level, control consoles faced inward, and little stairways, only a couple of steps each, bridged the path upward and inward. The difference in height between the innermost circle—where Captain Bataille was stationed—and the outermost ring where Mazel Rheun stood watching was only about one tall dog's height, but it created a weird psychological effect, placing the captain on a pedestal. Mazel's feline muzzle quirked into an amused smile. Shep would *love* that, she thought sarcastically.

Taking a deep breath, Mazel approached her old friend

and new captain. The large German Shepherd was focused on one of the central consoles and didn't see her approaching. She cleared her throat and said, "So, Reptassan architecture. That's what brings you out to this corner of the galaxy, right?"

Shep Bataille snorted and straightened up. Damn, he was tall now. Mazel stood as tall as she could herself, triangular ears pointed forward and paws clasped together firmly behind her back, trying not to shake as Shep eyed her.

"You're one of the new science officers assigned here," Bataille woofed. "Kind of a snarky first introduction to your superior officer, don't you think?"

Mazel blinked and said with the sweetest, most innocent voice she could manage, "Don't you recognize me? Your old friend, Rheun? I mean, I'm not a captain anymore since last we met... but..." She trailed off, unable to keep up the ploy while continuing to speak. Suddenly, the bright light beaming down from the ceiling felt very hot on her fluffy fur. She smiled coyly in a way that her new feline face could; as Darius, she could never have smiled so mysteriously, so knowingly. Jokes had always showed plainly on his canine face.

Bataille stared blankly for a few moments and then sputtered, choking out the words, "Darius??? Big Dog? Oh my heavens, it's good to see you!"

Mazel laughed, and some of the heat gathering in her fur dissipated. She'd never expected Shep to call her 'Big Dog' again. It felt good. Better than she could have imagined. Suddenly, she felt like herself again, even if her body was different in every way than the Rheun parts of her expected and her memories were longer and more complex than Mazel had been alive for.

Shep stepped closer, arms wide and head tilted to the side just enough to show he was asking if he could hug her. Mazel couldn't bring herself to raise her arms and reach out too, but she looked down, almost shyly, and nodded. Big canine arms wrapped around her, and even though the hug was all wrong —she was too low and too slight, and his arms wrapped all the way around her far too easily—it was also perfectly right, because it was Shep, her best friend, and he was exactly the same. And he had immediately accepted her.

When Shep stood back to look at her, his face broke into an easy-going, wolfy grin. He shook his head. "I should have known you'd show up here. You always were fascinated by the nexus passageways."

Mazel smiled again, this time wishing her face were better at naive innocence and less suited to mystery. Darius had never explained the connection between his Rheun chip and the nexus passageways to Shep Bataille or any other dog. He'd been a dog himself, and he knew how it would affect them, how it would make them weird around him. He hadn't wanted that. And he'd had an excellent poker face.

Fortunately, Captain Bataille didn't know Lieutenant Mazel Rheun well enough yet to see that she was hiding something behind her smile. "Yes," she said. "The nexus passages are fascinating, and I guess I've picked up a few new... I mean, held on to a few old..." Her ears splayed, nonplussed by her own internal disagreement about who she was—Mazel, a fresh young feline officer, or Rheun, an ancient neural chip passed down from one lifeform to the next over centuries of lifetimes. Finally, she settled for saying, "Studying nexus passageways is still one of my hobbies. Passions."

Shep's head was tilted again, watching her. "It's been a bit of a rough transition for you, hasn't it?"

Mazel straightened her ears and narrowed her eyes. The young cat in her didn't like Captain Bataille's unearned familiarity, and the old dog in her didn't like seeming weak in front of his friend Shep. But she wasn't a young cat or an old dog. She was both. Shep Bataille had earned the familiarity he was showing through years—decades, really—of friendship, and she was weak. She was a young lieutenant, confused by the process of integrating her two selves, and she should be grateful for her captain and friend showing compassion. "Yes. It's been rough. I..."

Mazel felt a wall she'd built up around her heart, to protect herself over the last few months, begin cracking. She'd lost all of her old life—both of her old lives, really. Mazel's family didn't understand how much she'd changed. And... she'd never even been to see Darius' family. She couldn't face meeting with Jebastion. Who was she to him now? She was no longer his father.

In a rush she said, "I barely know who I am sometimes."

Captain Bataille nodded seriously, slowly, ponderously.

And Mazel had time to doubt her choice to speak so openly and honestly about her weakness with a superior officer. And some of the wall around her heart sealed back up.

"But it doesn't get in the way of my work. That's the one thing," she said, defending herself, "that's remained constant. I was a scientist before, and I'm a scientist now. Darius wouldn't have chosen me to inherit the Rheun chip if we weren't fundamentally compatible." The words sounded better than they felt. It was a good story. She wasn't sure how much she believed it. She didn't know why Darius Rheun had chosen her. They'd barely known each other. Before. She knew him intimately now. Now that he was dead. But the logic of his choice still evaded her.

Shep waved a paw dismissively. "I know, I know," he said. "Don't worry. I wasn't going to relieve you of duty or refer you to the psych officer or anything. I know from your record as Mazel Tabbith—who I had been expecting—as well as your record as Darius Rheun that you're an officer I can trust with my life. That's the kind of officer I'll need in this wreck of a Reptassan space station."

"Thank you, Captain," Mazel said.

Now Captain Bataille drew a deep breath. His triangular ears flicked, and his gaze darted around the strangely shaped, overly hierarchical room. Canine, feline, and avian officers worked busily at about half of the stations; the other half of the stations were unmanned, display screens cracked or simply flickering. The elevator on the outer ring that led down to the next deck below command had appeared and disappeared, always empty, several times while they'd been talking. It was clearly malfunctioning.

"As you can see," Bataille said, "the Reptassans didn't leave their space station in good condition when they evacuated."

"You mean when we kicked their scaly asses out," squawked a nearby bird. Her feathers were blue and shimmery with touches of red and purple at her throat and wingtips. Her tailfeathers fanned out in an array of autumnal hues. She'd been working at the first officer's station, and she was beautiful in a way that made Mazel's feline heart skip a beat.

Mazel wasn't used to working around birds, even in her previous lives. For several lifetimes now, she'd been an officer of the Tri-Galactic Navy, the space fleet of the Tri-Galactic Union, and most of her fellow officers had been other cats and dogs.

The Tri-Galactic Union had been originally founded by the uplifted dogs and cats of Earth, and while other species they'd encountered in the three galaxies had joined the union, none of the most prominent races were avian. So far.

The Aviorans of the planet Avia, the world that the Nexus Nine Base orbited, had opened a petition to join the Tri-Galactic Union. That was why Captain Bataille was here; he was meant to shepherd their leaders through the complicated process. An appropriate role for a German Shepherd like him —he had always been a natural leader with a keen eye for the critical path to follow and a way of gently guiding others towards their own goals.

Mazel felt a sense of safety and security, knowing he would be her captain for the coming time. Maybe she could finally figure out who she was—not just the recent confusion of becoming Mazel Rheun, but perhaps she would finally uncover the origin of her Rheun-self, a quest that had consumed her since before the young cat could remember.

Mazel's Rheun memories stretched back through time like the view widening around a shuttle craft as it rises higher and higher into the sky. The more she concentrated on them, the farther back she could see. But eventually they darkened in the distance, like space enveloping her when the imagined shuttle craft broke free from the planetary atmosphere of her memories.

But no stars. She couldn't see the stars. Mazel Rheun couldn't remember where the Rheun chip had come from. Darius Rheun hadn't been able to remember either. Nor the bear, Augrula Rheun, who had preceded him. The oldest coherent memories any of them had been able to call to mind were full of tentacles and glass aquarium walls and an oval face framed by long hair. Before that, only fragments.

Rheun didn't talk about this memory with other cats or dogs. Especially dogs. The dimly remembered oval face would mean too much to them. Far too much. Sometimes, it meant too much to her, and the burden of being one small calico cat who knew so much of her people's history was overwhelming.

"Excuse me?" the blue-feathered bird squawked. She turned her head almost entirely sideways, looking at Mazel expectantly. She'd been talking, and Mazel hadn't been listening. She'd been lost in an infinitely deep feeling well of reminiscences.

"I'm sorry," Mazel said. "I was remembering something. What were you saying?"

The bird looked exasperatedly between Mazel and the captain. As she moved, the light flashing off of her feathers turned them more of a royal purple than their original rich blue. "Was she even listening to me?"

"Go easy on the lieutenant," Bataille said. "She's had a long journey to get here."

The bird's feathers bristled out around her head, making her larger for a moment before she managed to smooth them back down. Her uniform was a jewel-toned shade of purple, like her feathers had looked in the changing light. The other birds on the command deck all wore similar uniforms. The Tri-Galactic Navy cats and dogs—including Shep and Mazel —wore uniforms in more muted tones of black, brown, and slate gray. Mostly colors that came close to matching each individual officer's fur, as that made them easier to keep crisp and clean, given the problem of shedding fur.

"As I was saying," the bird repeated, "I'm Commander Neera Jerysha of Avia. I'm the attaché officer here on... *Nexus Nine Base* during the transition."

"Commander Neera is my first officer." Captain Bataille looked at the bird fondly, and she narrowed her bright-dark eyes at him. "And Lieutenant Rheun is a science officer here to study the nexus. She's also an old friend of mine."

Mazel could practically see the words *favoritism* and *corruption* pass through the Avioran's mind. She wanted to explain to the bird that their relationship wasn't like that— Captain Bataille wasn't asking for Commander Neera to treat his friends specially; he was simply telling her about the friendship in order to include her in the constellation of his friendships, a form of social consideration he afforded to all of his colleagues. Shep Bataille was a very friendly dog.

"Would you show the lieutenant around?" Bataille asked Neera. "Get her situated? A lot of the science stations onboard are still offline, but I'm sure there's some work you can get started on. And I'm sure you're eager to get started!"

"Yes, Captain," Neera answered with a head bob.

As the Avioran led Mazel away from the raised center of the command deck, down to the outer rings, Bataille called after them, "Come by my quarters later, Big Dog, and we'll catch up! Maybe grab some dinner on the esplanade."

"What's the esplanade?" Mazel asked Neera quietly, trying to sound conspiratorial, but the bird looked at her like she was a blithering fool, ruining the effect.

"I'll take you there," Neera said. "After I show you to your station up here. It doesn't work. Almost nothing does in this Viper's Perch. Plummeting Reptassans."

Mazel had read the standard briefing reports on the political situation regarding Nexus Nine Base during her flight into the sector, so she knew the Aviorans and Reptassans had been at war until only a few years ago. The two sentient species had evolved in different star systems, but the reptilian race had expanded out from their home star system and established space stations in several neighboring systems—including one in orbit of Avia—while their bird-like neighbors were still, metaphorically speaking, testing the wings of a brand new, experimental space program.

Perhaps, when you can fly through your own sky under the power of your own wings, there's less need to build metal mechas to carry you even higher. Or perhaps the reptilian people of Reptiss simply happened to stumble into sentience earlier along the galactic timeline than the bird-like people of Avia and thus had a head start on building space-faring technology.

Regardless, the Aviorans hadn't stood a chance when the Reptassans decided to invade and occupy their home world. Their only world. The occupation had lasted eighty-some years. Longer than Mazel, Shep, or Neera had been alive.

Mazel knew all of that. She'd read the words. But she hadn't been prepared for seeing the reality first hand. The dysfunctional, torn-apart space station; the hard-edged anger emanating from Neera and the other Aviorans.

"Here's your station." Neera gestured with a ruby-tipped pinion feather at a computer console with a cracked display screen, sparks flying from a bundle of ripped wires, and a toppled chair that was leaking stuffing from its slashed cushions. The bird lowered her head, peering closely at Mazel's reaction. From the new angle, her sharp beak looked longer and more imposing. "You got a problem with it?"

"No, it's perfect," Mazel said.

"Don't be condescending. It's junk," the Avioran retorted, kicking the toppled chair with a talon that looked suspiciously like the right size for creating the slashes in its cushions. "But I have it on good authority—well, insistent authority—that the fuzzy white guy over there who looks a lot like you--" She pointed at a West Highland Terrier with pointy ears and a shaggy beard who was up to his elbows in more ripped wiring underneath a different station. Mazel supposed that from a bird's perspective, a small white dog and a small calico cat with pale markings would look awfully similar. "--he's actually some sort of wizard and will have all of this working by Migration's Eve." She flapped her wings in an exasperated way. "I'll believe it when I see it."

Without looking away from the wires he was working with, the West Highland Terrier barked, "I can hear you doubting over there! And if you're just going to throw a lot of negative energy around this deck, you can get out of my way! Come back after your migration festival or whatever it is..." A spray of sparks shot from the wires, and the terrier yipped. Then he grumbled to himself about foolhardy, cold-blooded Reptassan engineers.

"The alleged wizard is Lieutenant Walker O'Neill," Neera said. "You can introduce yourself later. Let's get out of here." She led the way to the erratic elevator, and the two of them waited until the malfunctioning device decided, seemingly on a whim and not in response to Neera having summoned it, to come all the way up onto the command deck.

The ride down involved lots of stopping and sudden re-starting. But eventually they made it past all the decks of crew quarters and cargo holds down to the esplanade.

Neera hopped out of the elevator and spread her wings. "Welcome to the esplanade!"

CHAPTER 2
THE ESPLANADE

The deck they'd come to was wide and open, as large around as several city blocks and two stories high, with arching windows around the perimeter and even more windows worked into the floors, all looking out at the stars or the planet Avia below.

An expansive stretch of lacy white clouds shrouded the turquoise and jade crescent of the world currently in daylight. The wholesome brightness of the planet in its gemstone shades of green, blue, and pearly white only made the esplanade itself look shabbier. Outside the windows was natural wonder, large enough to spend lifetimes exploring; inside was a cramped, dingy space. Scorch marks seared across the window frames and marred some of the windows. Rubble was strewn about, including broken pieces of the esplanade itself—stairwells and walkways that should have provided a second level, wrought of some dark metal, had twisted and crashed to the floor.

At another time, in another condition, the esplanade might have been stunningly beautiful. At this moment, in this condition, it was only stunning for the story it told. A story of destruction.

And yet, Tri-Galactic Navy and Avioran officers worked together, clearing away the mess, repairing what they could.

"The captain wants to grab dinner here?" Mazel mewed. "How??"

Neera waved a wing apathetically at Mazel, gesturing for the cat to follow. The bird hopped her way through the rubble, between pillars and broken walkways. Mazel did her best to follow, staying light on her paws. They worked their way to the far side of the esplanade where a bar had been jerry-rigged together. Pieces of rubble had been arranged like chairs and tables.

Behind the bar itself—which looked like it might have been an actual fixture of the esplanade, that had only been scorched and not fully destroyed—a creature like a giant slug with tiny hands all along each of its translucent edges and four bulbous eye-stalks sprouting from its head seemed to be fixing drinks. Mazel recognized the creature as a Sliggurm.

"That's Scharm," Neera said, perching on one of the pieces of rubble. "When the food-synthesizer in your quarters malfunctions—and it will malfunction—Scharm's Bar is your best bet for something edible around here. Not good, mind you. But edible."

"Good to know," Mazel said, but she didn't take a seat. "Anything else you'd like to show me on this tour? Like the science labs maybe?"

Neera twittered, the chirpy avian of laughter. "Science labs? What kind of space station do you think this is?"

"One that the Tri-Galactic Union has requisitioned for studying Nexus Nine," Mazel answered primly. She was moved by the signs of what Neera's people must have faced in reclaiming this space station from their oppressors, but she was tired. She had traveled a long way and faced a challenging reunion. She wanted to return to the safety of something she knew, and what she was best at—what she had trained for—was studying unusual spatial phenomena like the nine nexuses.

Rheun had already visited and analyzed the previous eight nexus passageways that the Tri-Galactic Navy had discovered during previous lives. Mazel hoped to learn something new from this one. She hoped and had reason to believe this one would be different.

"Sit down, cat," Neera squawked. She whistled something in a high pitch that Mazel couldn't understand, and the slug-like Scharm responded by slurping its way over with two glasses.

Scharm set the glasses down in front of them, and Mazel sniffed the pink concoction. It looked like cough syrup and smelled like burnt sugar. "Is it alcoholic? Psychotropic?"

"Just nectar from the jumaria tree," Neera said. "The other Tri-Galactic Union officers have been lapping it up since they got here. It gives you energy. But no other effects."

"I could use some energy," Mazel observed. The drink had a sticky thickness on her tongue, like honey, and the flavor left an aftertaste of melon and lavender. It was fruitier than Mazel's usual milk-based choices, but she could probably grow to like it. A few moments later, the buzz of new energy hit her, and she revised her estimate: she already liked it. "Jumaria nectar," she said. "I'll have to remember that."

"No you won't. It's practically the only thing to drink up here. Half of the time you can't even get plain water."

"Why is the station still in such bad condition?" Mazel asked. "From the reports I read, the Reptassans abandoned it more than a year ago."

"They abandoned nothing," Neera said. Her voice seemed to have sweetened with the sweetness of the drink. She sounded almost like a songbird now. "We--"

"--kicked their scaly asses out. Right, right, I remember."

The bird's eyes twinkled in a smile. "That's right. But just because we kicked them out didn't mean we had the resources to make use of an orbital space station ourselves."

"But--" Mazel started. She stopped herself before she'd shoved too many paws in her muzzle though. Instead of arguing, she took another sip of the jumaria nectar and changed the subject. "I'm here to study the nexus that orbits your sun, just beyond the second gas giant. Can you tell me what you know about it?"

Neera's voice turned reverential, like she was singing an ancient song: "The Sky Nest has blessed our world with its protection for as long as we've recorded history."

"But have you studied it?" Mazel pressed.

"Constantly." The bird looked smug. "It is the home and voice of our gods, all in one."

Mazel was irritated. "That's a beautiful belief. But I mean, have you studied it scientifically?"

The cat and bird stared at each other over their sticky sweet glasses of nectar. A stand-off. Finally, Mazel decided to take a risk. She had lifetimes of Rheun's experience telling her to be cautious about extending friendship to new people and all of Mazel's confused youth—she was practically a kitten still—telling her that she needed to reach out. If she didn't reach out, then Neera couldn't reach back.

"Do you want to know why the captain told you to go easy on me?" Mazel asked, working hard to keep her ears from flattening against her head. Sharing private information about herself made her feel vulnerable and nervous.

"He told me," Neera squawked.

"He did?" Mazel asked, confused. When had the captain had time?

The bird shrugged. "You're friends. Like the captain said."

"Oh, no, that's not it," Mazel said. The small cat started shaking slightly. She hoped Neera didn't notice. "Actually, that was the first time I've ever met Captain Shepherd

Bataille. At least, in this lifetime. I've now talked to you more than I've ever talked to him. But I remember talking to him..."

"What do you mean?" The bird tilted her head, cautiously intrigued.

"Up until a few months ago, I was Mazel Tabbith. Just a cat in the Tri-Galactic Navy. Only a few missions under my belt since graduating from the academy. Then my commanding officer, a dog named Darius Rheun, died during a dangerous mission, and my ship's doctor told me that his will had selected me to be his successor."

"Successor?" The bird looked skeptical now, but she was still listening.

"Turns out the old dog had a neural chip implanted in his brain—that's Rheun." Mazel touched her paw to the base of her skull where she thought of the Rheun chip being. Then she moved her paw away quickly, as if she'd been breaking a social taboo by picking at an unsightly scab or maybe like her subconscious movement had revealed the location of a hidden treasure. She extended a claw and traced it around the rim of her jumaria nectar glass, trying to gather her thoughts. "Before my previous captain was Darius Rheun, he was Darius Benson. But I don't remember being Darius Benson... at least, not the same way I remember being Darius Rheun." She was babbling. "It's more like a memory of a memory..."

"What are you talking about?" Neera squawked. "Are you trying to distract me from something with this gibberish?" The bird twisted her head about, looking all around them, examining the other patrons of the haphazard bar. Her neck was far more flexible than a cat's or dog's. And her feathers danced in color between purple and blue as the light shifted over them.

This bird might not seem to like her very much, Mazel thought, but she liked this bird. Neera seemed tough and practical. She'd be a good ally if Mazel could only figure out how to connect with her.

Mazel tried to speak plainly, shoving past her jittery nerves: "The neural chip implanted in my brain has been passed down from one host to the next for many lifetimes. Part of me is the same young cat I was a year ago, but part of me has lived dozens of lives—some of them as other cats and also dogs. But also..." She trailed off. This was where she was taking a risk. The rest of her past was sure to become common knowledge around here, if she stayed long. But what she wanted to tell Neera next was a secret.

"Look," Mazel said, leaning forward, conspiratorial again, "have you heard the Tri-Galactic Navy dogs around here talk about the First Race?"

Neera didn't cooperate with Mazel's conspiratorial tone. The bird leaned back, stretched out her wings, and squawked in a louder voice than usual, "First Race, sure. That wizard, O'Neill, barks about the First Race all the time. What is it?"

"That's our religion—the most popular one on our home world."

Now Neera tilted her head, showing real interest. "Go on. All the dogs around here pretend like religion is beneath them, and they're somehow better than us Aviorans who believe we can see the home of our gods."

Mazel's muzzle quirked into an amused smile. She didn't usually hear dogs accused of thinking they were better; that insult was generally saved for cats. "The First Race is a phrase that refers to the first species on our home world to gain sentience—a breed of naked-skinned primates. They uplifted a variety of furry mammalian species to sentience after them."

Neera blinked her beady eyes. "You didn't evolve sentience on your own? You needed help? All of you?" Her voice was twittering with laughter by the end.

"All of us from the planet Earth," Mazel said. "And if you ask any dogs about it, they'll insist that humans—our First Race—probably came to your world by spaceship and placed the seeds for your sentience some time far back in your history."

The bird snorted. "Not likely."

"No," Mazel agreed.

The bird eyed the cat. Mazel imagined Neera was trying to figure out if she'd been drawing a parallel between dogs and their irrational beliefs and Neera's own statements about the Sky Nest. The bird must have decided it didn't matter, because she said, "What happened to these humans? Why haven't I seen any of them here?"

That wasn't the part of her history that Mazel wanted to talk about, so she kept her answer vague: "They're gone. But what I wanted to tell you is—my Rheun chip is ancient. So ancient. I don't even remember how far back the memories go... They get hazy..." She needed to focus. It was far too easy to get lost in reminiscences. She was too young to be this old. "But I remember being human once. Several times, actually."

"You remember being your own god?" Now Neera seemed really interested.

"They weren't gods," Mazel said. "They were just... people."

Mazel clasped her paws around the jumaria nectar glass. She downed the last of the nectar, and licked a few drops from her whiskers. All the while, Neera watched her carefully.

Finally, the bird said, "Oof, that's a big burden."

"I haven't told anyone in a long time," Mazel said. "Lifetimes. It doesn't usually go well when I do. They treat me differently. Especially dogs. Shep... the captain, that is... he doesn't know."

"You keep this a secret? Why did you tell... me?" The bird looked aghast.

"I wanted you to understand why I'm here," Mazel said.

"Okay..." the bird said. "I'm not getting it. Connect the dots for me."

"I have this neural chip in my head, and it's... who I am. I look like a naive young cat, but I'm also ancient, so ancient, I can't remember where I came from. Who built me? Why?"

Neera didn't say anything, but she looked entranced. She shook her head, opened her beak to speak, closed it again, and shook her head again. Finally, she said, "Those are big questions. Why did they bring you *here*?"

"One of my earliest memories involves travelling through a nexus passageway." The memory was dim, and only a fragment, but when Mazel focused on it, she could feel her tentacles coiling around her as she watched through a spaceship window—the space outside blossomed like a midnight orchid with velvety black petals, then exploded like fireworks. She knew viscerally that she was leaving her home behind and going somewhere new. That was it. The whole memory—tentacles, space bending outside her spaceship, and the sensation of leaving home.

Mazel pulled herself out of the memory and continued: "I've been to the previous eight nexus passageways that the Tri-Galactic Navy has discovered, looking for evidence that they're where I came from... But none of them matched up. I'm hoping whoever created me came from the other side of your Sky Nest."

"Lucky number nine, huh?"

"Lucky number nine," Mazel agreed. And she found it profoundly restful that Neera wasn't familiar enough with Earth culture to make a joke about cat's having nine lives. Mazel had lived a lot more than nine lives by now. Going by the old wives' tale, she should be long gone. And she'd simply heard the joke so many times before.

Mazel still cringed at the memory—very recent and fresh compared to so many others—of meeting herself for the first time. That is, when Mazel Tabbith met Darius Rheun—a memory she could recall from both sides now—her singular cat self had said, *"With all those previous lives, shouldn't you be a cat*?" Her neural-chipped dog self had sighed wearily. At the time, her cat self had felt clever, but now she regretted the easy, ill-considered joke immensely. Now she could feel directly how very little Darius had thought of her for it—just another snarky cat or dog in a long chain of them making the obvious joke when they first met him. Of course, Darius had gotten over his poor first impression of her. He must have, since he'd picked her to become him.

Mazel wished she could figure out how to access those memories, the memories where he'd changed his mind about her, but she couldn't seem to recall how Darius had come to think highly enough of her to select her as the next carrier of the Rheun chip. She could remember in painstaking detail spending hours worrying over which color of suit best flattered a coat of curly brown fur that she hadn't had in several lifetimes... but she couldn't find the memories she was specifically looking for.

Memory could be so frustratingly slippery and elusive. And memory had become such a big part of her life. She had more memories now than Mazel Tabbith would have ever been able to accrue during her one lifetime without the Rheun chip. With the Rheun chip, as far as Mazel knew, she was essentially immortal.

The bird finished her own drink, slammed the glass down, and said, "I can't tell if you're a lost youth who needs my help or a tired old elder who I should be coming to for wisdom."

"Neither can I," said Mazel.

Neera twittered in laughter. "Alright, well, we don't have science labs on this station—the Reptassans built it as a military base. Besides, I don't think those cold-blooded scale-tails are all that interested in science anyway, not unless it can build a better weapon. But I can set you up with some empty crew quarters as a work space, and you're welcome to try to requisition equipment from the Tri-Galactic Navy. If they sent you here to study the Sky Nest, then they'll probably support your research. I may have my doubts about Avia joining the Tri-Galactic Union, but one thing I have to admit about you triple-galaxy folks: you sure do love sending supplies. So, that's probably not the kind of science lab you're used to, but it'll be something."

"Thank you," Mazel said.

"Don't thank me yet; I'm not done," the bird snapped. "Besides, all of that is just what the captain clearly expected me to do for you anyway. I was just making you wait for it."

Mazel had known it was a good idea to get this bird on her side. Life on Nexus Nine Base would be a lot easier with her as an ally than as an enemy.

"Here's what you can thank me for—if it works. I'm going to talk to the Vee on this station—that's one of our religious leaders—and see if I can convince her to give you access to one of the Broken Twigs."

"Broken Twig?" Mazel asked.

"A broken fragment of the Sky Nest," Neera explained. "They fall to Avia sometimes. We've collected several dozen over the centuries. Several more have been found floating in space since we began exploring our star system. We store them in protective force shielding, and the faithful make pilgrimages to see them. Coming into contact with a Broken Twig has been known to cause visions. Our gods speak to us through them. The Broken Twigs are very important to us. Sacred. They must be treated reverentially."

Mazel raised a paw, pads toward Neera and claws carefully sheathed. "Reverential. Got it. I'd offer nothing less."

Neera nodded solemnly, accepting Mazel's promise. "Still, setting up a session for you with a Broken Twig could take some time, getting the proper permissions for an outsider and all. What I can do right away is introduce you to Omoleura. I think you two will have a lot in common."

"Omoleura!" squeaked a voice nearby. "Why would she want to talk to that bug?!"

Mazel blinked at the space the voice had come from and realized there was a frog-like creature with bulging eyes crouched on a piece of rubble at the next table over. The creature's skin and clothes were tinted to match the background behind him, making him very hard to see, but as Mazel watched, his color shifted to green. His chameleon-like skin was a standard evolutionary trait for some species; however, the suit to match must have been very expensive. He stuck out a hand with bulbous fingers.

"Quincy, at your service," the frog galumphed. "And anything you want done by Omoleura, I can get done for you half price."

Mazel shook Quincy's hand. The bulbous fingers looked slimy, but they just felt smooth.

"Get outta here, Quincy!" Neera squawked.

"Your wish, as always, is my command." Quincy's wide face split into a smile that Neera looked like she wanted to claw off with her talons. "But you should know this isn't the best place for sharing... *secrets.*"

"How much did you hear?" Mazel asked.

"Oh, nothing," Quincy said, oozing insincerity.

"Unless he wants to blackmail you later," Neera said. "This guy is all ears and bad deals."

"Ears?" The frog looked affronted. He gestured at his own face—all bulgy eyes and wide smile. No ears. "What do I look like? A Pollengi?"

Mazel laughed. She was familiar with the Pollengi—an avian race, halfway between turkeys and chickens, with large feathered crests on either side of their beaked faces. Their feathered crests did look a lot like giant ears, and those crests would look hilarious sticking out of Quincy's froggy face.

"But seriously," Quincy said, "I am a good listener, and if the pretty kitty needs someone to talk to later, I'm easy to find."

Neera glared at Quincy.

"When I want to be found, anyway."

Neera didn't stop glaring, but Mazel smiled as she watched the frog hop away.

"You weren't seriously charmed by that slime-ball, were you?" Neera asked.

Mazel shrugged. "A little. When you've lived as many lives as I have, you spend most of your time being too old and intimidating for anyone to risk flirting with you like that. Besides, I've never met one of his species before, and that's unusual for me."

"Long life with lots of memories, right." Neera shook her head. "Well, if you found meeting a Phiboon interesting, then you're going to love meeting Omoleura. There are hundreds of thousands of those conniving amphibious chameleoids from the swamp world Phibious hopping around the galaxy. There's even a half dozen of them right here in the Viper's Perch. Sorry, Nexus Nine Base." Her voice changed as she said, "But there's only one Omoleura."

Mazel wasn't sure what she was hearing in Neera's voice —reverence? Fondness? Something good though.

"I'll take you to zim," Neera said.

"Zim?" Mazel asked.

"Gender neutral pronoun."

"Oh, sure," Mazel said.

"Come on." The bird hopped up from her perch of rubble and set out, away from the bar. Mazel followed.

"Should we pay for the drinks?" Mazel asked.

"I have a tab with Scharm," Neera replied. "Don't worry about it. By the end of tomorrow, you'll probably have a tab with him too. Everyone here does."

As they forged their way across the esplanade, dodging work crews and especially dangerous pieces of fallen rubble or exposed wiring, Mazel noticed something happening in the sky, just beyond the horizon of Avia. The blackness of space bulged, sparkled, and then exploded in a series of brightly colored flashes that cut through the blackness in straight lines. The sight reminded Mazel of playing pick-up sticks as a kitten. She could see how the Aviorans had come to think of Nexus Nine as a nest in their sky made by gods and composed of mystical broken twigs.

"It's beautiful, isn't it?" Neera chirped from beside Mazel. The cat hadn't realized that she'd stopped walking, too awestruck by the nexus's beauty to do anything but stand and stare.

"It's different than the eight other nexuses I've seen," Mazel said. She glanced at Neera and saw the bird's feathers puffing up in a decidedly unhappy way. "Yes, I mean, it's breathtakingly beautiful. Of course. I just... I wonder why it's so different."

Neera looked mollified by Mazel's praise of the Sky Nest. The bird shrugged. "The Unhatched don't live in the other nexuses, I imagine. So, of course they're different."

"I suppose they don't," Mazel said, her whiskers rising in a smile. There was something peaceful about being friends with someone whose religious beliefs weren't directly contradicted by her own lived experiences. For all Mazel knew, there actually were trans-dimensional beings living inside the hyperspace folds of the nexus, and those beings did care about and speak to the avian lifeforms on the planet nearest to them. There really might be gods in the Sky Nest.

Truth be told, Tri-Galactic Union scientists knew very little about the nexus passageways. They'd sent dozens of unmanned probes into Nexus One before creating one with the proper shielding to survive the passageway all the way through to the other side. When the probe finally emerged on the far end, it had sent back readings through the nexus showing a newborn galaxy, burning far too hot and too dense to be safely explored. A dead end.

Mazel had been a different cat back then, also a scientist specializing in spatial anomalies. Karianne Rheun. She had a dim sense that Karianne had remembered more of why they studied the nexuses than Mazel knew now. Something she had forgotten during the intervening years. But she couldn't put her paw on what it was. Though she did remember the disappointment, the extreme disillusionment Karianne had felt when the far side of Nexus One turned out to be dangerously uninhabitable.

For a couple of lifetimes, Rheun had moved away from studying the nexuses directly, not wanting to feel the same disappointment. Instead, each incarnation of Rheun kept up on the literature, eagerly reading about the discovery of Nexuses Two and Three, but being only mildly amused and disdainful when the passageways turned out to lead to each other. The same happened for Nexus Four and Five. By Nexus Six, the Tri-Galactic Union had come to think of the strange hyperspace passageways as a series of freeways to be discovered for the purpose of travelling within the three inhabited galaxies more efficiently.

Rheun continued to hope for more, and when he became Darius, the dog returned to studying the nexuses directly. He uncovered a subatomic distortion created by travelling through a nexus passageway; an unmistakable trace, a fingerprint, that uniquely identified whether any particle had ever traveled through a specific nexus.

In this way, Darius knew for certain that the Rheun chip had not originated in the turbulently youthful galaxy on the other side of Nexus One and that his fragmentary memory of leaving home through a nexus had not taken place in the passageway between Nexus Two and Three or Nexus Four and Five. The Rheun chip showed no trace of ever having traveled through any of them.

When Nexuses Seven and Eight were discovered and found to lead to entirely unexplored galaxies, Darius joined in the joy of the scientific community. But he experienced the same personal disappointment as Rheun had with all the others—none of the first eight had left their fingerprint on the neural chip. None of them led to Rheun's forgotten origin.

Neera led Mazel back across the esplanade, pointing out useful landmarks like the Altar to the Unhatched—"It's only temporary, something the Vee on the station threw together so we'd have a place to worship. Just a small room with a few pieces of religious art and incense to set the mood. But then, I guess most things on the Viper's Perch are temporary. And sometimes temporary has a way of turning permanent." Neera shrugged her wings. They passed a few other points of interest—restaurants and shops being set up, mostly created by local Avioran merchants, hoping to appeal to the Tri-Galactic Union officers stationed onboard.

"A few weeks ago," Neera said, "this place was mostly abandoned—just a skeleton crew to keep it running. Then the prime minsters' council voted for us to petition to join the Tri-Galactic Union, and suddenly, I'm no longer the captain around here, and the Viper's Perch becomes Nexus Nine Base."

"Sounds dizzying," Mazel said. "I hope the captain has been listening to your input, since you clearly know this place better than any officer who only set paw aboard a few weeks ago could." Of course, Mazel knew the captain had been listening. Shep Bataille wouldn't be so foolish as to ignore a valuable resource—and potentially difficult thorn in his side —like Commander Neera.

Neera didn't reply, but the bird looked pleased; she seemed to like having Mazel take her side.

Finally they came to a formidable pair of sliding doors built into an archway. The doors slid open in response to their approach, and on the other side, Mazel saw a spread of computer banks showing video feeds from small, empty, numbered rooms—probably prison cells. Behind a desk in the middle of all of the computer banks crouched a being that looked, at first glance, like another Avioran. But something about the creature's smell was wrong—too sharp and zingy, not musty and sweet.

Mazel stepped closer and saw that while the overall shape of this creature was like an Avioran, the details were all wrong. Instead of actual feathers, the creature had thin fuzzy wings, and a coat of fuzz over its hunched body. Instead of a beak, it had a pointed pair of chitinous mandibles that mimicked the shape of a beak.

"Omoleura, I'd like to introduce the new science officer that the Tri-Galactic Union has sent over to poke and prod at our Sky Nest." Neera flapped a wing in the calico cat's direction and said, "Lieutenant Mazel Rheun." Then she flapped her wing toward the strange insect. "This is Omoleura, zhe's been the chief of security on the station since back before we kicked the Reptassans out. Sometimes the chief here was the only justice standing between the Avioran workers on the station and our Reptassan slavers."

The insect straightened up from zir hunched posture. "The Reptassans liked to keep things orderly. Justice is orderly." Zhe extended a many-jointed arm that had been folded against the underside of zir wing. The arm ended in a talon which Omoleura held out to Mazel. "I believe your people like to shake hands during introductions?"

"We do," Mazel agreed. She took Omoleura's talon in her paw. "It's nice to meet you."

Neera looked uncomfortable. The bird had not offered a wing for Mazel to shake when they'd met, and she tucked both of her wings behind her back now. Mazel hadn't been surprised or bothered by the Avioran not offering her wing. In Mazel's experience, winged sentients rarely liked shaking hands, even if their wings had evolved to have functional digits and work more like paws or hands than feral wings. At a deep level, a bird's wings are for flying free, and they don't belong clasped in a cat's paw.

"Will you be sending missions through the nexus

passageway to the galaxy on the other side?" Omoleura asked with a chittering, clicky voice. "If so, I'd like to join you."

"Captain Bataille will be in charge of those decisions," Mazel said. "I'll be analyzing Nexus Nine's subatomic distortion signature at first, and then the hyperspatial folding patterns."

"Fascinating," Omoleura chittered drily. Zhe didn't seem to speak from zir beak-like mandibles, but rather by vibrating the many-jointed legs folded against zir wings.

As Mazel looked at the insect, she realized the dark spots she'd assumed were eyes were nothing more than dark spots of fur, and a cluster of large multi-faceted eyes hid beneath the beak-like mandibles.

Mazel wanted to ask Omoleura about zir physiology and species' history, but they'd just met. And she didn't want to be presumptuous. So instead, she asked, "Do you have a particular interest in the galaxy on the other side of Nexus Nine?"

"I do," Omoleura replied, unhelpfully.

"Don't be difficult," Neera said. Apparently, being difficult was exclusively her job. "Omoleura believes zhe was brought to Avia by way of the Sky Nest."

Omoleura shifted zir wings in an unsettled way. As the thin fuzzy wings and the folded many-jointed legs underneath shifted, the difference between Omoleura's insectile mimicry and an actual Avioran's wings became more obvious. But then the difference melted away in stillness, and Omoleura looked like a bird again. Powerful camouflage. "I've never met another member of my species," Omoleura chittered, "or anything like my species. In the three galaxies, I seem to be unique."

Mazel could identify with that uncomfortable feeling.

Omoleura continued: "If I came, originally, from the other side of the nexus, then I would like to find my people."

Could the Rheun chip have been created by an insect race?

That was a possibility Rheun had never considered. Mazel didn't remember ever having a chitinous shell covered in fuzz or many-jointed legs or seeing the world through a cluster of multi-faceted eyes. Was it possible to forget an experience like that? She had clearly forgotten a great deal about her time as an octopus—she remembered being an octopus in an aquarium, studying the human scientist who thought she was the one doing the studying. She remembered revealing herself to the human scientist and choosing to pass her Rheun-self on to the human when her octopus-self died.

That's right—not only had humans not been the god-like beings dogs thought they were, they hadn't even been the first sentient lifeforms on Earth. There had been a thriving octopus nation deep beneath Earth's oceans for millions of years before humans came into ascendance on dry ground.

Mazel believed the Rheun chip had lived through millions of those years among the octopi, but she only retained a smattering of memories throughout them. And yet, in her memories the sensation of her own tentacles coiling, stretching, and clinging with their sucker discs held such a visceral, primal, powerful quality that Mazel had trouble believing she could have forgotten anything as equally strange as many-jointed legs and multi-faceted eyes.

Yet memory dims with time, and she could not be sure.

Perhaps Omoleura's and Rheun's origins lay in the same direction, but Mazel thought it unlikely that they were one and the same.

Before Mazel could say any of these thoughts—or rather, sort out her thoughts into which ones were safe to say—to Omoleura, the three of them were interrupted by the doors sliding open again. On the other side stood a gray squirrel in a Tri-Galactic Navy medical uniform, his bushy tail whipping around wildly behind him.

"Chief Omoleura!" the squirrel cried. "The medical bay has been robbed!"

Neera sighed dramatically. "Quincy," she squawked. "What did he take this time?"

"Let's not leap to conclusions," Omoleura chittered. After a drawn-out, creaking sigh of zir own, zhe added in a voice like a tuning cello, "Though the sticky-fingered Phiboon seems to be behind most of the petty theft around here." Omoleura turned zirself toward Neera in a way that must have been almost entirely decorative, since zir multi-faceted eyes surely had a wider view of the room than any of the rest of them. "Can we continue this introduction later?"

"Certainly," Neera agreed. "I just wanted to make sure that you and Lieutenant Rheun crossed paths."

The squirrel nearly jumped out of his fur. "Lieutenant Rheun? Lieutenant Mazel Rheun?" He rushed up to Mazel and looked the calico cat up and down. He was a big squirrel, and she was a small cat, so she was only a hair taller than him, pointy ears to pointy ears. He held out a delicate paw toward her, but he didn't wait for her to take it. Instead he suddenly clasped both of his paws around one of hers and squeezed tightly. "I'm Doctor Elijah Jardine, and I'm so excited to meet you! Boy, I bet you could really tell some interesting stories!" His tail fluttered behind him.

Mazel didn't know what to say to the pretty but overeager squirrel. Clearly, he'd read her medical record, and he knew about the Rheun chip.

"Oh, no, I'm sorry!" He covered his muzzle with both paws, and his tail straightened stiffly. "I shouldn't be..."

"It's alright," Mazel said. "Commander Neera already knows about my... unusual history, and we were about to tell Chief Omoleura."

The squirrel looked immensely relieved.

"Though I guess I know better than to tell you any secrets," Mazel jibed.

Jardine's jaw fell open, and he worked it several times, seemingly trying to come up with a response. Finally, he nodded demurely. "That's more than fair," he said. "I deserve that. Nonetheless, I would love to buy you dinner some time, and hear stories of the days of yore!"

"Days of yore?" Neera repeated with a tone of shock or disgust.

Mazel had to admit, the phrase was a bit much, but it amused her. Everything about the little doctor seemed to be a bit much. Though she supposed that a squirrel would have to be a determined fellow to work his way through the ranks of dogs and cat in the Tri-Galactic Navy.

"Come, Doctor Jardine," Omoleura chittered, "I think it's time that you give me your report..."

With no further prompting, the bright-eyed, bushy-tailed squirrel launched into an in-depth, extremely detailed description of his discovery of the missing supplies, beginning with his breakfast that morning. He was a very handsome but overly loquacious fellow, Mazel thought.

Meanwhile, Neera gestured with one wing for Mazel to follow her, and with the other she made a sweeping gesture at Omoleura that seemed to imply she'd check back with zim later. Then the bird backed out of the chief's office.

Once they were back on the esplanade, sliding doors shut behind them, Neera said, "That doctor has been one emergency after the other since he got here. Pretty tail though. Not quite like the tails on the rest of you Tri-Galactic folk...?" She left the sentence hanging, halfway between a statement and a question.

"He's a squirrel," Mazel said, filling in the blanks for Neera. "The rest of us here are probably all cats and dogs. There are a variety of uplifted species from the planet Earth, but cats and dogs are the most prevalent in the Tri-Galactic Navy."

"Huh," Neera said. "What about the really big fellow?" She arched her wings out and hopped on her talons, trying to look larger. "Kind of hulking and husky. Eh, I don't know, maybe she's a dog too. Just a really, really big one."

"Could be a bear?" Mazel suggested. There weren't any uplifted bears from Earth—humans hadn't gotten to uplifting bears before the Dark Times and their disappearance—but there was a species of Ursines in the Tri-Galactic Union who'd evolved sentience naturally on their own home world of Ursa Minuet. Mazel remembered her time as an Ursine very fondly. It had only been a single lifetime, but oh what a lifetime! She would enjoy meeting another bear aboard Nexus Nine Base.

Mazel shook her head to clear it. Any bear here wouldn't be "another bear," because Mazel Rheun wasn't a bear.

Neera led Mazel back into the malfunctioning elevator, and they rose several levels into the decks of crew quarters. As promised, Neera set Mazel up with a pair of conjoined, empty quarters for her to turn into a science lab to supplement the simple work station in command.

"There's a standard computer bank, food synthesizer, and a cot that I suppose you won't need," Neera said. "We can have someone fetch that out of your way." The bird looked pensive for a moment. "There's probably someone else aboard who needs it... Reptassan living quarters tend to be spartan, especially, I imagine, on a military base. They were never much for creature comforts while they were busy subjugating and overworking us."

"This is great," Mazel said, hoping to extricate herself from the conversation before hearing too much more about the Reptassans. She wanted to be friends with Neera, but she'd had a long day full of new—and new to her—people. She needed a chance to unwind. Alone. Well, as alone as she could ever be now that her mind buzzed with memories of other lifetimes. Sometimes it felt like her previous selves were speaking to her, judging her, advising her, or just commenting on every little thing. She knew what each of them would have thought. Sometimes, it was hard to pick her own thoughts out of the mess. "I can get started with this."

Neera left Mazel to her multiplicitous self, and the cat went straight to the computer. She spent a couple of hours researching the overlap between the scientific equipment she needed for her studies, the equipment that was readily available, and the equipment that was most likely to interface with the Reptassan hardware on this station. She'd never had to design her own science lab before. It was partly fun and freeing, like putting a puzzle together without any rules to follow for how to do it. But it was also daunting, and in the end, a little depressing.

Rheun had worked in first-class laboratories all across the three galaxies, and what Mazel was throwing together here would be a haphazard, jerry-rigged, stop-gap measure of a lab at best. But it would get the job done. And she supposed, even the world-class laboratories she'd worked in had had to start somewhere. It was a sign of respect for her scientific work—as both Mazel and Rheun—that the Tri-Galactic Union had put her in charge of this operation, entirely by herself.

Of course, it was also a sign of the political unrest in the system. The Tri-Galactic Union didn't want to devote too many resources too quickly to a backwater system recovering from nearly a century of war. Technically, Nexus Nine belonged to the people of Avia, and their religious beliefs could interfere with the progress of scientific research if Mazel wasn't careful.

Once Mazel's requisition orders were sent off to the nearest Tri-Galactic Union base, she curled up on the thin cot that Neera planned to take away. The cot was beside a window looking out on the star-studded space outside. There was no window in Mazel's personal quarters, but the cot was exactly the same. Besides, Mazel wasn't sure she could find her own quarters without help right now, or maybe just some sleep first.

CHAPTER 3
RESEARCHING THE
SKY NEST

Mazel dreamed fitfully of her past lives. Her body changed from small and fluffy to gangly and short-furred, leaving her wobbling and off-balance, then her long, canine legs stretched like taffy being pulled until they became coiling tentacles. Dogs and cats who had been close to Rheun but had died years ago—or hundreds of years ago—whispered to Mazel, saying words she couldn't quite hear. Mazel woke abruptly from the dream, startled awake by the sensation within the dream of her tentacles calcifying into chitinous legs that only bent in a few places. More places than her feline legs. But so few compared to the infinite bending of a tentacle.

Her heart raced. And her shoulder ached from the hardness of the cot. If she found her way back to her own personal quarters, she could unpack the bags she'd brought to Nexus Nine Base with her and maybe sleep better. She had a patchwork quilt that she'd sewn as a kitten, a bonding project with her father who liked sewing and had wanted to teach her. Each patch had come from fabric cut out of clothes she'd loved but outgrown or scraps she'd bought with her allowance during trips to the fabric store. The quilt was plush and comfy and full of memories—but quiet memories that stayed nicely in their own pieces of fabric rather than reshaping the inside of her mind.

Mazel would sleep much better curled up in her beloved blanket. But she was awake now, and she decided to start her day early. She wanted to start finding answers.

Mazel used the food synthesizer to summon a simple breakfast. Well, she tried to, anyway. The breakfast she programmed into the synthesizer was piping hot pancakes with sunny side up eggs on top. The breakfast that actually sparkled into existence inside the synthesizer looked more like a weird scrambled egg breakfast casserole—the eggs and pancakes had been all mixed together into a mushy pastiche. Neera had warned Mazel that the synthesizers were likely to malfunction... She sent in a request for repairs.

The eggy maple confection didn't taste as bad as it looked, so Mazel picked at it while sifting through all of the data she could find stored on the station's computers about Nexus Nine.

The scientific data was limited—ninety years ago one of the first Avioran space flights, Wing One, had passed through the nexus and returned safely. The pilot of Wing One swore she'd experienced visions of the Unhatched during her time flying through the nexus, which she referred to as the Sky Nest. Wing One's shipboard computers recorded star patterns on the far side of the nexus that guaranteed the passageway led to an entirely different galaxy, not one of Tri-Galaxies.

Mazel spent some time trying to pattern match the astral configurations from Wing One's recordings to any of the star patterns in the two new galaxies that had been discovered beyond Nexus Seven and Nexus Eight, called Efta and Octo, respectively. She had no luck. Of course, Wing One had stayed in the foreign galaxy beyond Nexus Nine for less than an hour total, and the recorded data was extremely limited.

Mazel couldn't completely rule out that Nexus Nine led to

either Efta or Octo. She tried to remember that, even if Nexus Nine led to Efta or Octo instead of a sixth galaxy, it could still be the nexus passageway she remembered, dimly, passing through in her far, far past. And Efta and Octo had barely been explored by the Tri-Galactic Union so far. She could still find her origins in one of them.

But Mazel hoped that Nexus Nine led to a galaxy that hadn't been explored at all before. Fresh and brand new. Or maybe, deeply familiar. Maybe... home.

Mazel shook her head to clear the strange thought from her mind. Her home didn't lie on the far side of any nexus passageway, no matter what her studies uncovered. Her home was on Earth with the parents and littermates she'd grown up with. In this lifetime. She couldn't let the weight of memories subsume who she was now.

An unpleasant, atonal chime emanated from the door, and when Mazel went to check, she found Lieutenant O'Neill—West Highland Terrier and alleged wizard—flanked by two Avioran officers in the corridor, each of them bundled up with arms full (or wings full) of equipment. They even had a trolley behind them, loaded up with equipment as well.

"This isn't everything you requested," O'Neill barked, barging his way into the quarters. The Aviorans followed him, pulling the trolley behind them. "In fact, some of it, you didn't request at all." O'Neill placed a big mechanical box on the cot where Mazel had slept. The Aviorans followed suit. She wouldn't be sleeping there again any time soon.

O'Neill continued explaining, as he sorted through the equipment: "But we had some scanners delivered for your lab before you arrived, and then some of this stuff is cobbled together from Reptassan left-overs and Quincy's black market operation. I know, I know, TG-Union doesn't do black market--" He held his fuzzy white paws up defensively. "--but Nexus Nine Base is weird and different, and I'm just trying to bandage this open wound of a space station into working, any way I can."

"I won't tell," Mazel swore.

The Aviorans helped get all of the equipment off of the trolley, and then O'Neill dismissed them. The terrier and cat were left alone, surrounded by towering piles of scientific devices, none of them operational.

"I'll be working on your lab all day," O'Neill said. "Getting everything set up and working. Any requests? As to the order I install these in? Or where any of it goes?"

"Anywhere it fits," Mazel answered, already having reconciled herself to losing the cot. She would need to find her own quarters before tonight.

The terrier looked around the plain quarters, perhaps gauging whether there would be enough power sources or whether he'd have to do rewiring. "These are really nice quarters," O'Neill mused. "Large. And most of them don't have windows, but then I suppose you need to be on the outer edge of the ring to tap into the station's main arrays. And First Race knows you need the space!" The ramshackle, uninstalled equipment had already filled most of it, wires and power cords dangling from them with potential.

"While you're here," Mazel said, "you should know that the food synthesizer was malfunctioning earlier."

"Not surprising," O'Neill observed. "Good to know, though, since I'll be installing a number of these power hungry devices into the synthesizer. It's the perfect power conduit, but I'll definitely want to get it fixed first, so it doesn't fry them with unpredictable surges."

This meant no more snacks in the lab. Mazel sighed. She really would have to find her own quarters. She thought about asking O'Neill if he could change the horrifying atonal sound of the door chime, but compared to everything else happening, it just seemed too trivial. She needed to get used to a certain level of discomfort on this retrofitted Reptassan station.

The terrier went to one of the walls and began removing screws from a panel. Once the metal panel came down with a teeth-gritting screech, he dug his paws deep into the wiring inside, quietly swearing to himself the whole time about cold-blooded engineers and their tail-backwards designs.

Mazel could see she wasn't going to get any more work done in the lab today. Too many distractions. She down-loaded everything she could find in the station's computer tagged with "Wing One" or "Sky Nest" into a port-screen and excused herself. O'Neill didn't seem to notice her leaving.

Mazel wandered the corridors of Nexus Nine Base for a while, familiarizing herself with the sinuous layout. The corridors coiled back and forth, doubling back on themselves more than on a Tri-Galactic Union designed space station, and the doors were set back from the hall in intimidating arch-ways. Everything was built out of dark materials—slate gray, steel gray, gun-metal gray. But the lights were bright, almost like heat lamps. Mazel's creamsicle and white fur and pale uniform reflected the yellow light fairly well, but the bright-ness soaked into the dark gray walls and floor, radiating back out in an oppressive warmth.

Cold-blooded architecture, Mazel supposed.

Eventually, Mazel found her own quarters—#347. The number was posted clearly beside the door, but she hadn't yet discerned the pattern governing which order the numbers were in. Once inside, Mazel laid the port-screen with her reading material down on the cot and got to the business of unpacking. She only had a few bags. Tri-Galactic Navy offi-cers were encouraged to travel light. In space, every gram counts. Besides, most useful objects could be synthesized when needed.

Mazel spread her patchwork quilt over the cot and synthe-sized a couple of fluffy pillows to go with it. Well, she tried to.

The pillows came out lumpy and flat. Still, better than nothing.

Mazel placed her few sentimental mementos around the room—a confusing mix of pictures and knick-knacks from her childhood as Mazel and precious objects saved from previous lives. She had a flute that she'd never played with her current body and a curved sword, much too large for her. But each of them had traveled with her for longer than Mazel had been alive. She hung them on the bare walls with hooks from the synthesizer. At least those came out right.

Mazel's precious souvenirs from her most recent kitten-hood felt strangely cheap and shallow in comparison to the gravitas of these objects that had belonged to her for lifetimes but had barely touched her paws in the brief time since she'd inherited the Rheun chip. These were the objects that had survived from one host of the Rheun chip to the next, deemed important enough to be kept even though they'd belonged to her when she'd been someone else.

Mazel lay on the cot and read the port-screen. She discovered that most of the material she'd downloaded was Avioran scripture and scriptural analysis. Religious writings. She should have expected that. The nexus was a religious icon to the Aviorans, and everything they wrote about it had been filtered through that lens.

Nonetheless, there was a lot to be learned from the Avioran writings—they'd been studying the nexus faithfully for as long as they'd had language. The information had to be translated from poetry into data, but the data was still there.

Specifically, she knew that the nexus had been appearing in their skies for centuries; she knew it appeared irregularly. Sometimes the Sky Nest appeared multiple times in a year, and other times, it stayed dormant for decades.

Mazel knew from researching the other eight nexuses that the passageways were generally only visible—with their brightly colored fireworks-like displays—when something passed through them. Of course, the object passing through a nexus passageway and triggering its photonic exhibition could be anything from fully crewed spaceships—or fleets of them—down to particles of space dust.

Since there was no record of aliens from a distant galaxy descending on Avia, Mazel imagined that most of the Sky Nest's appearances could be chalked up to space dust. There might be an unusually thick cloud near the passageway.

The atonal door chime rudely interrupted Mazel's scientific musings and shook her out of her reverie. When she answered the door, she found Captain Bataille on the other side, bearing an opened flagon of peanut butter beer.

"I didn't know if you'd still like the stuff," Bataille said, shifting the flagon between his paws nervously. Peanut butter beer had been Darius' favorite.

Mazel wanted to say, *"Of course! I still love it!"* But she knew the yeasty brew wouldn't agree with her. And she'd spent enough months confused by her own choices, unsure of what she really wanted, that she'd had to develop guidelines. And number one on the list was—no matter how much she'd enjoyed eating something in a previous lifetime, she needed to respect the body she lived in now. And Mazel didn't care for beer.

Bataille's triangular ears flicked back; he could sense her hesitancy and was reacting to it. The ease that had existed between Mazel and Bataille yesterday was slipping away, and Mazel was desperate to hold onto it. Shep was her anchor here. As long as he knew her, she knew that she hadn't totally lost herself by coming here. Because Mazel Tabbith would never have accepted—let alone *requested*—this mission.

"I don't drink beer anymore," Mazel admitted. She checked the time on the port-screen that she was still clutching in her paws. The time was much later than she'd expected—she'd spent all day reading about the Sky Nest. "But you know, I'd love to get some dinner and catch up like you suggested yesterday." She tucked her port-screen into one of her uniform's pockets.

"Let's do it," Bataille woofed. "After you." He gestured for her to lead the way.

"You don't want me leading the way," Mazel said as she stepped out of her quarters and into the bright light of the hallway. She'd dimmed the lights in her quarters for a more muted, peaceful atmosphere. "We'd never get anywhere. I spent ages wandering through these decks this morning before I found my way back to my quarters. I'm seriously thinking about synthesizing up a loaf of bread so I can leave bread crumbs to lead me home. I'm just worried about--"

"--what the synthesizers will actually give you." Shep laughed. "Yeah, Lt. O'Neill has been busy since I got here fixing broken synthesizers. It's like a blasted whack-a-mole game."

Mazel wondered how well that phrase would hold up if the Tri-Galactic Union ever discovered a race of sentient moles. Not well, she expected.

"Yeah, yeah, I know what you're thinking," Bataille said. "And I'll drop 'whack-a-mole' from my vocabulary the very minute I meet one. Okay?"

Now Mazel laughed. "You did know what I was thinking," she marveled.

"Sure, I did." Bataille began striding down the corridor with his long legs, but he quickly adjusted his pace when he noticed Mazel was having trouble keeping up. "We've only been friends since we were puppies, Big Dog."

"But... does that mean I was only thinking it because Darius would have?" Mazel wondered.

"Hah, oh my, you sound just like Darius used to after getting the Rheun chip from that bear--"

"--Augrula. I loved being her."

"Right," Bataille agreed. "That's what Darius always used to say too. She sounded awesome. Regardless, I'm going to tell you now the same thing that I told you back then." Bataille stopped and turned to look Mazel directly in the eyes. He tucked the flagon of peanut butter beer under an arm and placed a large paw on each of her shoulders. "You are my friend. You are yourself. No matter who that self is--" His muzzle skewed into a lopsided grin as he adjusted the words. "--she is awesome, and I feel lucky to know her."

Mazel nodded, trying to take the words in. They were familiar in a deep way. They were words that had pulled her together a lifetime ago, before she'd even been born. "Thank you. I knew I needed to come--" She wanted to say "home to you." Instead she said, "--be near you. I knew that serving with you would steady me."

"My pleasure," Bataille said, leading the way down the hall again. "Now what was this about not finding your way back to your quarters until this morning? I don't have officers sleeping on the bulkheads, do I?" He shot her a leering grin. "Or did that charming squirrel doctor make a big impression on you?"

"Oh goodness," Mazel said. "He is quite something, isn't he? Though he comes on a bit strong." This was better. This was the comfortable give and take that she expected from her best friend.

"Well, I know he would have turned Darius' head," Shep said. "I'm just not sure if you have the same type."

"Honestly, I'm not sure either," Mazel said. A year ago, she knew exactly what type of tomcat she liked. There was nothing that made her swoon more than crisp stripes that came into adorable little Vs right above bright green eyes. And thick white whiskers sprouting out of dimpled dots of dark fur on a paler muzzle... Oh, just the thought of such a tom made her feel all faint and fluttery. She'd had crushes on a series of just such toms during her kittenhood schooling and years in the academy.

And yet... Now she had memories of fifty-year-long

marriages; deep, long-lasting, complicated loves. Why, she'd met the love of her life more times than she could count on her claw tips. And those beloved life partners had ranged from short to tall, husky to bony, fluffy to short furred... and when she remembered far enough back, smooth skin and even tentacles...

Mazel could feel her heart skip when she remembered the faces of each of them. Red fur and floppy ears; shaggy blonde curls and a big black nose; clear blue Siamese eyes. Each one had changed what she found attractive.

One of them was still alive.

"Have you talked to..." She couldn't bring herself to say her husband's name with a mouth that had never kissed his.

"He contacted me, shortly after you... Darius... died," Shep said. "He said... to look out for you. He knew you'd come to me."

Mazel smiled sadly. "He knew it before I did. Is Jeb..." She choked on her son's name.

"He's okay," Shep said. "Sad, of course. But he sends me updates. He won an award for his latest science project in school and wanted to show it off to Uncle Shep."

"Good for him." Mazel stiffened her whiskers, refusing to let the wave of emotion overtake her. She was young. She'd never had a son. She didn't have a husband. She had... memories.

Another one of the rules she'd had to make for herself— but she'd made this one lifetimes ago—was that she didn't go back to romantic relationships from previous lives. It almost never went well. It wasn't fair to her new selves... or her old beloveds.

Mazel Rheun was a different person than Darius Rheun, and she couldn't step back into his life like he hadn't died. But she could continue her friendship with Shep.

"Buck up, Big Dog," Shep said. "They know the deal. No

one's expecting you to run home and fold yourself into a family that Darius started before Mazel was born."

"I'm not *that* young," Mazel objected.

"I'm saying that you're not a delinquent father," Shep said, suddenly serious. "I know Darius worried about that a lot, and who could blame you—him—given what his dad was like. But Darius was a great father. And now... you're done being a father. For now, anyway." Shep bumped his arm against Mazel's much lower shoulder in a friendly, jostling way. "I don't know what Mazel's plans are. Care to enlighten me?"

They came to the elevator, and this time it slid into place smoothly and promptly, almost as if it were actually responding to Shep pushing the button for it.

"Did O'Neill have time to fix that since yesterday?" Mazel asked, ducking Shep's bigger question about her life plans.

"He fixes it every day," Shep answered as they stepped into the elevator together.

As they descended toward the esplanade, Mazel found herself identifying with the wonky, temperamental space station and also the dog who kept fixing it. She had to fix herself every day too. Maybe some day, the fixes would take, and she could just live through a day without figuring herself out from scratch all over again. She remembered times in her life—her long life, the one lived by Rheun—when the trail of memories following her had felt like a blessing instead of a burden. She tried to believe those days would come again.

The elevator doors opened onto the esplanade, and dark metal walls were replaced with star studded vistas. The progress that had been made overnight was stunning. There was still rubble, but it had been gathered into piles along the walls. Scorch marks had been scrubbed away. And a couple of the little shops had been decorated with brightly colored silken banners.

"This looks better," Mazel said, impressed.

"Of course it does," Shep agreed, leading the way toward Scharm's Bar. "This is going to be the next big destination for Tri-Galactic Union research soon. A central hub of activity! It's got to look the part."

"Yeah, but how did you..."

"I leased a portion of the esplanade to Quincy," Shep said. "It's unorthodox, but blasted if that Phiboon doesn't know how to get things done! He hired a bunch of Aviorans and sub-leased sections out to others. He'll take a cut of the profits from most of the shops around here."

"Why not put an Avioran in charge?"

"None of them wanted the commitment. Most of them hate this place," Shep said.

"Right, the Viper's Perch." Mazel tucked a paw into the pocket with her port-screen and touched the device, thinking about everything she'd read about the Avioran's beliefs.

Instead of Scharm's Bar, Bataille directed Mazel toward a hole in the wall behind a draping, blue, silk curtain. "Do you still like Ursine food?" he asked.

"I think I do..." Mazel answered. In all honesty, she hadn't eaten any Ursine food since changing. And Mazel Tabbith hadn't eaten Ursine food ever. So, she wasn't sure. "I... I don't know. But... I'd like to try?" She remembered Ursine food as being rich and meaty, coated in crispy, honey-soaked skins, and served on beds of wriggling worms. She didn't know how she felt about eating wriggling worms anymore... but the crispy, honey-soaked skins sounded delicious.

An Ursine man dressed in what looked like a suit of chainmail armor showed the captain and Lieutenant Rheun to a table, one of only five in the establishment. It was a small place, and the only windows were on the floor beneath their feet. Blue silk draped over all of the walls, and combined with the bright, warm lights, the effect had a sunshine feel—blue skies over a black sea. Except the sea stretched down forever. And the restaurant was only a small collection of lifeboats, rafted together and adrift on the ocean.

The Ursine man took their order—Mazel let Shep do the ordering, except she asked for a glass of sardine wine—and then disappeared into the back, leaving them to talk. They were the only patrons in the restaurant, so while Mazel knew better than to tell secrets on the esplanade—since apparently Quincy could be anywhere—she felt comfortable and safe talking openly about her life over the last year.

Shep was careful whenever he talked about Darius' family; Mazel could tell he was trying to feel out how much she actually wanted to know. He respected that she needed her distance. At least for now. Perhaps later, when she was more settled into being Mazel Rheun, she could find a way to connect with Darius' son. A new kind of connection. She would like—eventually—to be Jebastion's friend, and not lose him completely from her life.

For now, though, she settled for listening to Shep's second- hand tales. She was proud of that boy. Jebastion would be a good friend to have. Some day.

If he wanted to be friends with a cat who was a little older than him but remembered being his father...

"Rheun?" Shep said.

"Yes?" Mazel looked up from the plate of meat and wriggly worms that she'd been idly poking with her extended claws.

"You were drifting again," Shep said. "That's all."

"I seem to do that a lot these days." Mazel tried to smile, but she could feel that it didn't reach all the way to her whiskers.

One of the silky blue curtains drew back, and Commander Neera stepped through with a creature Mazel hadn't seen before. It looked almost like another cat with pointy ears and fuzzy white and orange splotched fur, but it moved wrong, too stilted and jerky, bending in slightly the wrong places. The effect was eerie and unnerving.

"Who's that?" Mazel asked the captain.

"With Commander Neera? That's the local chief of security," Shep answered. "Zhe's been the chief of security here through three administrations now—the Reptassans, Neera's Avioran skeleton crew, and now mine. I've been trying to convince zim to work with Tri-Galactic Navy officers, but zhe's very set in zir ways and has a retinue of Avioran officers zhe prefers working with."

"Wait, you can't mean Chief Omoleura..." Mazel said, staring harder at the creature. She could believe this strange creature was another insect, but it didn't look at all like Omoleura. It didn't have noticeable wings, instead favoring a more mammalian-style bipedal stance. And its face was... weird; like Mazel's own feline face, right down to her asymmetrical markings, had been shakily hand-painted on a piece of creamy white velvet and draped over a lumpy head. But definitely not beaked. Yet... a cluster of multi-faceted eyes were tucked away, nearly hidden beneath the creature's chin in exactly the same way as Omoleura's had been.

"But..." Mazel stuttered, struggling with reconciling these two wildly different insects. "I met zim yesterday... zhe looked..."

"Like an insect camouflaged as a bird?" Shep prompted. "Yes, zhe usually looks that way, but zhe changes from day to day."

"Really?" Mazel's voice lowered to a near whisper as Neera and her friend came closer. "Then how do you recognize zim?"

Omoleura approached their table and raised zir arms— each feline-looking arm seemingly constructed out of two multiply-segmented insectile arms held close together, all covered with creamy white and orange fuzz. Mazel found herself wondering how many different uniforms Omoleura had to keep in order to fit zir extremely changeable body. Or did zhe synthesize a new one every day?

"Because I'm unique," Omoleura declared, vibrating zir pairs of insectile arms that in concert looked like singular feline arms. As long as Mazel didn't look too closely. "If you see someone on the station who... doesn't fit. Doesn't look like anyone else. Doesn't quite... belong--" Omoleura spun around, nearly dancing. "--then that's me! Chief of Security Omoleura! One of a kind!"

Neera twittered in amusement. She seemed extremely fond of the unusual insect. "I see the captain has shown you where the high-ranking officers hang out after hours." Neera directed her statement to Mazel, but she nodded curtly at the captain. "Mind if we join the two of you?"

Shep took a moment before answering, making sure to catch Mazel's eye and measure her response. But Mazel was happy to spend more time with the crusty bird. Neera intrigued her, possibly even more than the bizarre chief of security who was seemingly imitating Mazel today.

"Not at all," Shep said.

Omoleura and Neera each grabbed a chair from the neighboring tables, all of which were still empty, and pulled them up to Shep and Mazel's table. The Ursine waiter—possibly the chef and owner too, given how small the place was—came over and took their orders, chainmail suit clanking with his every move.

Soon the four officers had a feast on the table between them and the place still to themselves.

Neera ate none of the meat, but she eagerly accepted all of the wriggling worms that Mazel didn't want. So the cat dumped her pile of worms onto the plate of the bird. Omoleura ate delicately, almost nervously, like zhe was waiting for the others to look away before taking dainty nibbles at the honey crusted meat. Mazel could understand why—zir face split open sideways in a pair of mandibles, completely destroying the illusion of felinity.

After her glass of sardine wine had been refilled twice and the conversation had ranged far and wide, Mazel finally blurted out at Omoleura, "Why do you look like me? Yesterday, you looked like Neera, sort of, but now... why me?"

Omoleura put down the piece of meat zhe'd been nibbling on, straightened up, and seemed to draw a deep breath... except, Mazel didn't think Omoleura breathed in the same way as birds and mammals. "I don't know," the insect answered at long last. An anti-climactic answer.

"I'm sorry," Mazel said, abashed. "Was that a terribly rude question?" She rushed on, a little too tipsy to wait for the answer: "I wouldn't have asked outright like that, except I think sardine wine affects me differently now that I have this Rheun chip in my head..." She held the glass of opalescent wine up to the light and swirled the oily liquid around. "I do love it though. And sometimes I just want to feel like myself, you know? My old self."

When Mazel looked away from the wine glass, all three of the others were looking at her, not saying anything.

"Maybe you don't know..." she said, mostly to Omoleura. "If you change so much, even more often than I do... was there ever a time when you felt most like yourself?"

"I feel most like myself these days when I look like an Avioran," Omoleura answered. "I feel... discomfited when I change into something as new--" Zhe gestured at zirself. "--as this."

"New?" Mazel's ears perked up in surprise. She couldn't imagine that mimicking any of the other Tri-Galactic Union cats—or small dogs—who'd been on Nexus Nine Base for the last few weeks could be all that different from mimicking her. Neera had barely been able to tell her and Lt. O'Neill apart. To Omoleura, they must look at least as similar.

"It used to be," Omoleura said, leaning back from the table, giving zirself a little more space, "that I'd go into a chrysalis and change into a new form every time I met a new creature. When I was very young, it didn't even matter if they were sentient. Just one day after the other, new form after form. Every night, I'd..." Omoleura hesitated, seemingly judging whether to proceed. "I don't know how graphic I should be."

Mazel blurted out, "They had to cut my skull open to shove the Rheun chip into the slimy gray folds of my brain. I was able to watch the whole thing in a mirror while they did it. Totally conscious, brain exposed to dry air. Couldn't feel a blasted thing."

"I think what Big Dog's trying to say," Shep said, "is go ahead and be as graphic as you like."

Neera shrugged her wings. "I've heard it all before. Plummeting winds! I've even seen it. You can't creep out me."

Omoleura's faux face couldn't smile, since it was constructed of differently colored patches of fuzz on a stiff exoskeleton, but zhe shifted zir double legs in a way that seemed to show greater comfort. "It feels like my insides turn to liquid... and I spit up silk, so much silk. I think it really is my insides, melting and reforming into a chrysalis shell that I spread over myself. Then I sleep. By the time I wake up, the chrysalis shell has grown brittle and breaks open. When I emerge... I'm someone new."

Omoleura's multi-faceted eyes seemed to glint at Mazel, and the insect added, "I mean, I look like someone new. On the outside. On the inside, I always feel the same. I can't even imagine having my mind combined with another mind, full of lifetimes of memories."

Mazel sat up straight, the fur on her shoulders bristling under her uniform.

"No offense meant," Omoleura droned.

"None taken," Mazel said, trying to understand her own reaction and sort out her complicated feelings. "I mean, I can't imagine being like you either. Having my body change like yours does, frequently, unexpectedly, and out of my control? That sounds terrifying."

"It is sometimes," Omoleura admitted. "But it's not entirely out of my control. Not any more. That's why I was so surprised to go into a chrysalis last night. I hadn't been planning to."

"You plan to?" Shep asked, nudging the conversation back into motion when it lulled, like any good sheep dog would.

Neera seemed unconcerned by the sudden awkwardness at the table, and Mazel was caught up in her own musings.

"Oh, yes," Omoleura said, answering the captain. "If I don't go into my chrysalis every so often, I get all stiff and brittle. I'm no good for anything that way."

"I think," Mazel said, letting her thoughts trip out of her mouth almost before she'd formed them, "that I was bothered by the idea that you can't imagine being like me... because in some ways, you seem more like me, living through all those changes, than anyone else I know."

"I feel the same way!" Omoleura exclaimed, seemingly so excited that zhe shifted zir entire body in a way that completely destroyed the illusion of zir camouflage, distorting the illusion of felinity entirely. "I think that's why I went into my chrysalis last night and came out this way. When Jerysha told me about your Rheun chip..." Omoleura settled back into the semblance of a calico cat, mirroring Mazel. "...I just hadn't felt a connection like that with anyone before. I hoped... maybe you'd be someone who could understand me."

"Well, I can understand that feeling," Mazel said. She held her glass of sardine wine up and gestured with her other paw, indicating Omoleura should raise zir glass of fizzing green liquor. When zhe did, Mazel clinked their glasses together. "Cheers," she said.

"Cheers," Omoleura responded in a cheerfully cello-like tone.

"Oh! It's like this poem in the *Book of the Unhatched*," Mazel exclaimed, remembering one of the passages of scripture she'd read earlier that day. She recited, carefully, making sure to get each word exactly right: *"Though some may swim through waters deep, and other run over grasslands quick, let those in the sky remember, wings are not flight—flight is different unto each who experiences it. Flight is freedom."*

"That's beautiful," Shep said.

"Is it right?" Mazel asked Neera. The bird looked stunned, and Mazel was worried she'd accidentally butchered a sacred piece of scripture. Or worse, maybe she shouldn't have been quoting it at all. Maybe only priests—Vees—were aloud to speak the Book of the Unhatched aloud.

"It was perfect," Neera said. "I just..." She tilted her head. Her feathers looked especially blue in a room draped with blue silk all around. "I didn't expect you to know it."

"I've been studying the Sky Nest," Mazel said. "I want to be respectful with my studies."

Neera nodded solemnly and folded her wings behind her. The conversation drifted on, but then suddenly, out of nowhere, Neera squawked, "I'll take you to talk to the Vee tomorrow. We can't bring a Broken Twig to the station, but if I vouch for you, the Vee can get you a session with the Twig of Foresight at the Temple of Yunib. We'll need to borrow a shuttlecraft to get down to the surface."

"Done," the captain said. Then he raised a paw. "If I can come. I've been hearing about these Broken Twigs since I got here, and they sound fascinating."

Neera agreed, and the party broke up shortly thereafter. They would all need a good night's sleep if they were going down to Avia in the morning.

CHAPTER 4
FLYING DOWN TO AVIA

The flight from Nexus Nine Base down to the surface of the planet took twenty minutes, and it was spectacularly beautiful. Lacy clouds streamed past the shuttle's windows, and the world below expanded from a globe of gemstone brilliance hanging in the dark sky into a vista engulfing them, bright blue sky all around and rich green expanses growing wider and closer below.

It was the kind of view that never grew old, even in a thousand lifetimes. Mazel would know.

"Why are we flying again?" asked Lieutenant Libby Unari, a black cat who'd joined the captain, Commander Neera, and Mazel on their field trip. She was another scientist, though her area of specialization was biology with a focus on botany. She'd requested a post on Nexus Nine Base specifically to study the plants on Avia.

Neera's feathers ruffled, though she stayed focused on piloting the shuttle as she answered: "The Temple of Yunib is under an anti-teleportation shield. We needed to protect our sacred places from the Reptassans during the occupation." The bird didn't seem to like the black cat much. Though Mazel wasn't exactly certain that Neera liked her much either.

The only person Neera seemed unequivocally to like was Omoleura.

"Yes, that makes sense," Unari agreed. "But the Reptassan occupation is over now..."

Neera eyed the black cat levelly before shaking her head and returning her focus to flying the shuttle.

As they got closer to the ground, the emerald and gold expanses of forest and field resolved into clearer details. They flew over cities dense with spire-like buildings; villages of thatched-roof cottages; and patchwork fields of agriculture. They flew away from the city centers, towards the unchecked wilds. Finally, they came to a crater, a broad gash in the earth filled with a lake. In the middle of the lake, a tiny island was set like a jewel.

Neera landed the shuttle inside the crater, on the narrow shore between the cliff edges and the clear, blue water. She led the others out, and when they were all standing on the sandy strip of shore, Neera handed each of them a shawl.

Mazel turned the shawl over in her paws—it was made from midnight blue fabric with intricate beading. The shawl looked handmade, not synthesized. Although, with the right synthesizer and a patient programmer, Mazel supposed it could have been quantumly fabricated into existence.

"Put them on," Neera said. "They tie around the neck."

Bataille fumbled with his, the delicate strings evading the manipulation of his large paws. Neera helped him. Mazel and Lt. Unari had no trouble.

In the sunlight, the beads glittered, and the shawls split in the back. Like wings. Mazel wondered if the shawls for her, Shep, and Unari were supposed to be substitute wings—a way to make outsiders acceptable on sacred land.

Then Neera pulled out a shawl of her own and affixed it over her own back with the deft motions of extreme practice. Her shawl looked much like theirs, but the fabric was faded and tattered around the edges. Old. Worn. Well-loved.

"These shawls represent the wings of the Unhatched," Neera said. "You must accept their purity and lightness into your heart in order to ascend to their temple."

"Excuse me," Unari meowed, "but I came along to study the strain of bonsai trees kept inside the temple, and I wasn't told anything about accepting a new religion. I don't even believe in the First Race!"

Neera looked surprised. "Aren't you married to the white dog who's always talking about them?"

"Just because Walker is a believer doesn't mean that I am," Unari snapped, trying to untie the shawl from her neck and snagging her claws.

"Stop," Neera said, placing a wingtip over the black cat's scrabbling paws. "Leave the shawl on, and you can come into the temple. The shawl is a symbol. You cannot enter the temple without it. However, whatever is or is not inside your heart, is a truth that lies between you and the Unhatched. If the shawl is a lie, only the Unhatched will judge you." And yet, Neera said the words with a tone that made it completely clear she would judge Unari as well.

Unari sniffed and let her paws fall from the tangled strings. The shawl stayed on her shoulders, draped over her uniform. "Fine," she said. "Purity and lightness."

"Purity and lightness," Bataille agreed. "I mean, really, who could argue with that?" The German shepherd cut through the tension with his wolfy grin.

Unari smiled back, and even Neera's eyes twinkled.

"The Unhatched are very wise," Neera said. "We would never have survived the Reptassan occupation without them."

"How so?" Unari asked, clearly trying her best not to sound antagonistic. "The hope and comfort of believing in them?"

Neera strode away from the others without answering, hopping down the beach. She came to a pile of driftwood, lifted one of the pieces, and pressed a series of buttons on a control panel hidden underneath. Moments later, a small boat rose out of the lake, water dripping from its sides. "No," she said. "They sent practical help—Broken Twigs from their Sky Nest. That's what Lt. Rheun and the captain have come here to see." She hopped into the boat and gestured with a wing for the others to follow. "Even without experiencing the Unhatched first hand through a Broken Twig vision, you will still see their beauty and wisdom reflected in the way that the Vees tend to the sacred bonsai trees. Though I'm guessing you'll mistake it for nothing more than quixotic cultural prac- tices and happenstances of evolutionary biology."

"That's quite likely," Unari agreed, stepping onto the boat. The black cat didn't seem at all offended, although the bird had clearly meant to offend her.

The boat wobbled under Mazel's paws as she stepped aboard, and then it lurched under the addition of Captain Bataille's weight as he stepped aboard behind her. Each of them sat on a wooden plank, and Neera pulled out an extend- able oar for each of them that had been stored under the planks.

"We're rowing?" Unari asked. Her whiskers drooped in disappointment. Mazel wasn't thrilled either, but she knew better than to show it.

"Nothing like a bit of brisk exercise on a beautiful day!" the captain barked, trying to keep the group's attitude light and positive.

"We row," Neera said, staring daggers at the black cat, "to show our willingness to work for the grace and wisdom that the Unhatched will bestow upon us in the temple."

"That's beautiful," Bataille said, dipping his oar into the water. "Deep and wholesome."

"Also completely made up." Neera began rowing in time with the captain. "We row because the anti-teleportation shield interferes with most technology near the temple. That's it. No symbolism."

Lt. Unari's muzzle quirked into a reluctant half smile at Neera's self-effacing humor. "I can see why Walker likes you," she said.

"Does he?" the bird seemed surprised. Mazel wasn't. Lt. O'Neill had seemed like a classic dog to her, the kind who liked everybody.

"Oh, yes, he says that the station would probably have fallen apart long ago if it weren't for you." The black cat's green eyes sparkled when she was talking about her canine husband.

Mazel wondered how long Lt. Unari and O'Neill had been serving together, and if they'd met before joining the Tri-Galactic Navy or after. Perhaps they'd met at the academy. A lot of relationships began during academy years, when the stresses were more abstract and theoretical.

Mazel imagined that balancing two careers in the navy together must be difficult, and yet it seemed so much easier than she could picture a relationship ever being for her. She knew that her previous selves had pulled off long term relationships... Surely, it would get easier to imagine. This would all get easier, and she would spend less time feeling dizzied by her past lives.

As they rowed across the lake toward the island, clouds flitted across the sky, thickening and darkening until the sunlight broke into scattered showers. Raindrops caught in Mazel's whiskers, making her nose twitch.

Lt. Unari's triangular black ears flattened, but she didn't complain. Captain Bataille turned his long muzzle to the sky and laughed. Neera seemed totally unaffected by the rain; the droplets literally rolled off of her feathers. Mazel had been thinking of the Aviorans as songbirds, but suddenly she wondered how closely related they were to ducks. Certainly their beaks were sharper, and their talons didn't seem to be webbed.

Mazel was tempted to ask about Avioran evolutionary history, but she didn't want to get something started between Neera and the biologist in the boat. The other cat and bird had already shown themselves to have enough spark between them without her helping to fuel the fire.

They rowed in silence, accompanied by the music of the rain.

When they arrived at the island's shore, a bird in impressive red and gold robes that offset her blue feathers and a crown-like headdress on her brow met them with wings wide.

"Welcome to the Temple of Yunib!" the bird twittered in a melodic voice. Definitely songbird-like. "I am Vee Wya, and I'll be curating your visit to the Broken Twig of Foresight. We are honored by your visit here to commune with the Unhatched and heartened--" Here the bird folded one wing over her breast. "--to know that the political leader sent to our world by the Tri-Galactic Union has more than mere politics in his heart."

Vee Wya helped them out of the boat, which they left beached on the sand. Then the Vee led them toward the base of the temple. To Mazel's eyes, the temple looked more like the scaffolding for a building under construction than a finished building itself. Yet the bare beams were decorated with hanging tapestries, carefully painted with scenes much like those Mazel had seen in stained glass windows from ancient Earth churches. The tapestries darkened with rain spots and fluttered in the slightest breeze. They must have been made from weather resistant fabrics.

"We keep the Broken Twig in the highest spire of the temple," Vee Wya explained as she led them through an arching doorway. On the other side of the doors was a courtyard, and the walls had so many open windows in them that Mazel barely felt like they'd entered a building at all.

"The Vee is saying there will be a good deal of walking," Neera warned.

The Vee's eyes twinkled merrily. "We stay in good shape here, climbing to the skies to commune with our gods and then returning to the ground to commune with our world twenty times a day. I trust the stairs won't be a problem for you?" The Vee's head bobbed as she seemingly took the measure of her guests.

"Not at all," the captain agreed.

Mazel remembered how positively Neera had responded to her quoting a single piece of scripture last night, and she searched her memory for something appropriate. Fortunately, the Rheun chip's greatest skill was remembering things. Mazel found the words slipped over her tongue easily, "When your wings beat weakly, remember that the body is to be ascended, but do not stop beating your wings at all, for there is no greater use of the temple of your soul than to rise upward in the joy of movement."

"Ah," the Vee said, spreading her wings wide, an impressive gesture on any Avioran, but even more so with the Vee's draping robes. "I see we have a student of the Unhatched here. Wonderful!" The Vee caught Neera's eyes and nodded in approval, seemingly pleased that Neera had chosen an appropriate acolyte to bring to the temple.

Neera's feathers puffed out in response to the Vee's approving nod. The commander looked quite proud of herself, and maybe also of Mazel.

As the Vee and Neera began discussing the scripture Mazel had quoted, Lt. Unari wandered away from the group.

The black cat seemed magnetically drawn toward a row of tiny ornamental trees displayed in colorfully glazed clay pots. Each tree seemed to be an entirely different variety, and they were arranged as a progression—from needled evergreens to small-leaved deciduous to broad-leaved succulents.

The black cat's green eyes gleamed at the sight of the trees, and Mazel could have sworn that the other cat was indeed seeing the beauty and the wisdom of the Unhatched— whoever or whatever the Unhatched were.

Lt. Unari approached an Avioran, in simpler robes than the Vee's, who was leaned over and tending to one of the tiny coniferous trees. The black cat asked something which Mazel couldn't hear, and the Avioran turned toward her, straightening up, and revealing her face.

Mazel gasped at the sight of the Avioran's face—instead of blue feathers, this Avioran had pebbly green scales around her beak and between her eyes. From what Mazel could see of the Avioran's wing tips, tail feathers, and the crest of feathers on her head, the rest of her body looked normal for an Avioran. But the scales on her face were far more reptilian than bird-like.

Mazel hadn't met any of the Reptassans yet in person, but she was pretty sure that she was looking at a mixed-species individual, partially Avioran and partially Reptassan.

Lt. Unari beamed at whatever the mixed Avioran was telling her and then came running back. "Excuse me, captain, Vee Wya, would it be alright if I stayed here with--"

"My name is Isstis." When the mixed Avioran spoke, her voice hissed more than twittered, and Mazel could have sworn she caught sight of a forked tongue.

"--Isstis, yes," Unari continued. "She's generously offered to show me all of the bonsai trees and teach me about them."

"Most certainly," the Vee said. Turning to Isstis, she added, "In fact, why don't you take cuttings for our visitor? I'm sure she'd like to take them back up to Nexus Nine Base and study them more in depth."

"I would!" Unari exclaimed, clasping her black-furred paws together.

Mazel noted with interest that the Vee hadn't stumbled over calling the space station by the Tri-Galactic Union name for it. Neera seemed to struggle with that every time.

Vee Wya led Mazel, the captain, and Neera to a spiraling staircase with a worrisome lack of walls or handrails.

As they began to ascend, Neera tweeted quietly to the Vee: "Is that wise, Vee? Lieutenant Unari is unlikely to care for the cuttings as sacred vessels of the Unhatched's generosity. She'll probably cut them into pieces and feed them through gene-mapping machines."

Mazel watched the Aviorans climbing the stairs ahead of her. The birds' talons grasped grooves built into the steps as they ascended. Cat and dog paws weren't designed that way. Though Mazel did extend her claws, trying to steady herself, but the steps were built from metal that her claws couldn't grip. She wished her arms had long pinion feathers like the Aviorans'—they were clearly using their wings for balance too. She felt so unsteady on these stairs, but as they climbed, the view of the island and the lake around them expanded, growing more and more spectacular.

"My fledgling, we each study the wisdom of the Unhatched in our own way," Vee Wya said. "Science is not at odds with my religious beliefs." She tilted her head and eyed Neera ascending the stairs beside her. "Is it at odds with yours?"

"Of course not, Vee!" Neera exclaimed, losing a step and falling behind.

For the rest of the climb, the three visitors from Nexus Nine Base listened quietly while Vee Wya told the history of the Broken Twig of Foresight. Although, Mazel got the sense that Neera was struggling against herself to keep from inter-rupting the Vee to add details to the story.

The Broken Twig of Foresight was the newest Broken Twig on Avia. The Twig had been found orbiting Avia and was first claimed by the Reptassans on Nexus Nine Base—which the

Reptassans had called Sesserak T'ih. The commandant of Sesserak T'ih, a Reptassan named Sukast, had looked into the Broken Twig and been granted a vision of Reptassans dying by the millions—their scaly hides splitting down the middle, sloughing away, and leaving nothing but a pile of loose feathers inside, feathers which had blown away on the wind.

Commandant Sukast had been so shaken by his Twig vision that he'd begun seeking spiritual guidance among the Aviorans he kept enslaved. He brought one Vee after another up from Avia to Sesserak T'ih and asked them what the vision meant. One after another, the Vees answered that the Unhatched would only forgive the Reptassans if they recognized the fundamental similarity between all sentient creatures, represented by the feathers inside Reptassan skin, and that they must leave Avia, restoring Avioran independence and freedom.

One after another, the commandant threw the Vees into the Sesserak T'ih prison cells, displeased with their answers. Supposedly, the commandant's orders grew increasingly erratic as the images from his Twig vision ate away at him. One after another, he made mistakes. And one after another, the freedom fighters took advantage of the growing opportunities to thwart him.

Supposedly, the discovery of the Broken Twig of Foresight led directly, tangibly to the Reptassan commandant's downfall, and when the Avioran workers took control of the Viper's Perch, the war on the planet's surface below finally turned their way.

After many, many flights of stairs, the Vee led them into a room with a panoramic view, only slightly obscured by fluttering tapestries on every side. They were at the highest point of the Temple of Yunib. The room was open to the elements, enclosed only by arching beams that gave the room, oddly enough, the feeling of a birdcage.

A ledge all around the edges of the room made the space

feel far more secure to Mazel than the twisting spiral stair-cases had felt. And she found a certain thrill in looking out at the lake from so high above, feeling the fresh, cool air and all of its movements in her whiskers. She even loved the feel of the ceremonial shawl on her shoulders, lifting slightly in the breeze. It felt a little like having actual wings, or so Mazel imagined. In all of her lifetimes, she'd never had wings.

Cats may not have ever been able to fly, but they do love high places. Captain Bataille looked much more nervous and unsure of himself on his large paws, tiny shawl flapping behind him.

In the middle of the room, Vee Wya lifted an ornate, gem-encrusted, golden dome from a raised platform. She set the decorative dome aside, and held her wings over the distorted, twisting, kaleidoscopic image of space-time underneath. A force field sparkled around the distortion, protecting them from it—or protecting it from normal space-time.

Reflexively, Mazel unholstered the uni-meter at her hip, flipped it open, and tried to scan the distortion. But her uni-meter was dead.

"Most technology doesn't work here," Neera said. "Remember?"

"Right..." Mazel re-holstered the uni-meter in frustration. Fortunately, she had a less powerful, antiquated, hand-held scanner that she kept in one of her pockets. It had belonged to her when she'd first joined the Tri-Galactic Navy... lifetimes ago. And Rheun had continued to carry it, for good luck, ever since then. Mazel pulled the antique scanner out and found that it did work.

"How old is that thing?" Captain Bataille asked, marveling at the ancient piece of technology.

"Older than your great-great-grandparents," Mazel said. Turning to the Vee, she asked, as respectfully as she could, "May I scan the Broken Twig of Foresight?"

"Be my guest," Vee Wya said, lowering her wings and

stepping aside. "Though I believe you'll find the Unhatched are much more forthcoming to those who seek their visions directly."

"And I would be honored to do so," Mazel said. "After I've reached out to them in my own way." She scanned the distortion that danced before her eyes like a trick of the light, like an optical illusion, like someone had scratched a gash in the face of the universe and space-time was leaking out through the crack.

Then she lost herself in the numbers that danced over her scanner's screen. She wouldn't be able to tell from this scanner's limited abilities whether the Broken Twig of Foresight came from a nexus that her own neural chip had passed through. Its computational abilities weren't powerful enough for that degree of complex pattern-matching. But it could store the raw data necessary for her to find out once she returned to Nexus Nine Base... as long as there was a science laboratory available for her when she got there. She hoped Lt. O'Neill had finished setting the laboratory up for her.

"Are you ready?" the Vee prompted, gently.

Captain Bataille put a large paw on Mazel's shoulder and said, "You can analyze the data when we return to the station. Would you like to go first? Or scan me while I go?"

Mazel hesitated, her scientific caution battling with her all around curiosity. As a scientist, she wanted to scan the Broken Twig's effect on Bataille before subjecting herself to it. But... She'd spent hours reading about the visions granted by the Broken Twigs, and she wanted to experience one herself. She wanted... She hoped... Maybe it would tell her that she was about to find her origins. Maybe it would show her origins to her directly.

"I'll go first," Mazel said. She handed the antique scanner to Bataille. "Make sure the scanner is running. I want everything recorded."

"Of course," Bataille agreed, balancing the small piece of electronics in his large paws.

"What do I do?" Mazel asked the Vee.

Vee Wya pulled a stool up to the platform and invited Mazel to sit on it. When she did, the Vee said, "I'm going to extend the force field protecting the Broken Twig to envelop you inside it. You'll feel a slight tingling as the force field passes through your body, and then--" She clapped her wings together, hopping as she did so. "--the Unhatched will share their foresight with you! So exciting! *Always* exciting."

"You look like a fledging on her hatch day!" Neera said, also looking pretty excited.

"Every vision is a gift from our gods, my fledgling," the Vee admonished Neera, suddenly serious again. "Let us begin. Stare into the Twig."

Mazel glanced at the captain and saw he was scanning her. Then she let her gaze fall into the roiling void of space-time in front of her. It was like staring at the edge of a water-fall, watching the water suddenly change direction, folding itself in response to the gravitational shape of the ground beneath it. Except space-time was the water, and the ground... was something deeper, something impossible to understand, something Mazel's scanners couldn't pick up.

Mazel felt the tingling sensation of the force field pass through her body, tickling her whiskers and then passing out through the back of her head and finally her tail tip. Her heart raced with anticipation.

But nothing happened. She stared harder at the crack in space-time where the universe was folding in upon itself and draining into an obscure hyperspace. She stared so hard that her eyes watered; her ears and whiskers flattened. But she saw nothing more strange than the crack in space-time itself.

Eventually, the tingle of the force field passed through her again, from tail-tip to whiskers this time.

"What did you see?" Neera squawked, overcome with excitement.

"Nothing..." Mazel said. She felt like a failure, even though she didn't believe in Neera's gods, and she certainly couldn't control the physiological effects of a rip in space-time on her brain.

"Nothing, like, everything gets destroyed?" Neera asked in horror.

"No," Mazel said. "Just... I didn't see anything. Nothing like a vision. I felt the force field pass through me, but then nothing happened." She felt profoundly, strangely disappointed, and she could see both of the birds eyeing her skeptically, warily, as if she might be a demon. "Maybe it doesn't work on mammals?" she asked. "Here, let me see the scans?"

Mazel reached toward the captain, and the German Shepherd let her have her antique scanner back. But the readings were inconclusive. Of course. There was a reason the scanner was an antique—they made much more powerful scanners now.

Mazel sighed. "Why don't you try it, Captain?"

The German Shepherd squatted down awkwardly on the tiny stool, legs akimbo and tail wagging excitedly behind him. Vee Wya began adjusting the settings for the force field, and the sparkly sheen of blue progressed through the air toward Captain Bataille, ballooning outward, reshaping itself into a bubble that could encapsulate him. When the sheen of force field touched his nose, Bataille's tail stopped wagging. He sat statue still, the fur above his eyes quirked into expectant eyebrows.

Once the captain was entirely enclosed in the bubble of sparkly blue, he closed his eyes, and a peacefulness crossed his face. He looked like he was dreaming, eyes twitching ever so subtly, and tail drifting through a slow motion wag. He looked like gods were speaking to him.

Mazel glanced back and forth between the captain and the

readings on her antique scanner, trying to make sense of what was happening, but she simply didn't have enough data. Eventually, she gave up on the scanner. It would store whatever data it collected for later. For now, she watched the captain as he dreamed.

After only a few moments, surely less than a minute, Vee Wya adjusted the force field's controls again. The blue, sparkly bubble shrank back down to a sphere enclosing the Broken Twig of Foresight and nothing more.

Captain Bataille opened his eyes.

Mazel couldn't bring herself to ask what he'd seen. If he'd seen anything. She wanted to believe the Twig experience didn't work for mammals—perhaps the Unhatched only spoke to those who had been hatched? Aviorans and Reptassans both laid and hatched from eggs.

"What did you see?" Neera breathed.

"Give our visitor a moment to recover, my fledgling," Vee Wya admonished.

But the captain said, "It's all right. I..." He shook his head, flapping his triangular ears. "I don't understand it, but I want to tell you." He looked at the Vee, his eyes full of wonder or confusion, seemingly seeking her guidance. "I was surrounded by people I've known... some of them gone many years now. My father. My first captain."

Captain Bataille glanced at Mazel. At first, she thought he was trying to share the feeling with her, trying to connect over a post that he and Darius had been assigned when they were first cadets. Then she realized, the captain was thinking of Darius himself. The Great Dane she'd been in her last life had appeared in the captain's vision.

"They spoke to me," Bataille said. "They called me... the Apex."

Both birds gasped, and the Vee took a step back. Neera hopped forward.

"The Apex?" Neera asked. "Are you sure?"

"They kept saying it, over and over again." The captain shifted uncomfortably on the tiny stool. "*Apex*. What does it mean?"

Mazel had seen references to the Apex in the scripture she'd read about the Sky Nest, but she hadn't read about the Apex directly.

Vee Wya shuffled forward, lifted the ornate golden dome from where she'd left it on the floor, and covered the Broken Twig of Foresight, hiding its disturbing space-time machinations from sight again.

"There must be a mistake," Vee Wya tweeted primly. "Could you have misheard them? You must have misheard them."

"I know what I heard." The German Shepherd stared levelly at the fancily robed bird. "What's the big deal?" he barked, voice raising. "What's the Apex?"

Neera's beak hung open and her gaze kept darting toward the Vee, as if she wanted to speak but couldn't contradict her religious leader.

Mazel said, "From what I read, the Apex is a figure in Avioran mythology. A messiah who will lead the Avioran people into a new era." She couldn't remember anything more. She hadn't focused on the passages that mentioned the Apex, because they'd seemed more like morality tales and fairy stories than poetically phrased history. In her mind, she'd classified the Apex with First Racer tales of humanity returning from the stars; the stories from Ursa Minuet of a Honey Golem who would train all righteous ursines in battle before their judgment day; and ancient humanity's traditions involving Santa Claus.

"An era of peace and enlightenment," Neera said, softly, reverently. She seemed lost in a world of deep thoughts.

The Vee's feathers ruffled, irritably, and she turned away to gaze out at the faraway cliffside beyond the lake. Even her tailfeathers splayed in a disorderly array.

"You mean, like an era of membership in the Tri-Galactic Union?" Bataille asked, rising from the stool and moving to stand beside the Vee. "I mean... I am here to help lead the Aviorans into joining the TGU." He broke into a jovial laugh, probably trying to break the tension. His tail wagged in the way it did when he wanted very much to please someone. "But I have to say, I'm no messiah!"

"No, you are not," the Vee snapped. All of her warmth and welcoming seemed to have melted away, and she looked terribly discomfited to be standing beside a canine who was more than a head taller than her. "Is this a hoax?" She turned aggressively toward Mazel. "Did you read up on our scripture and plan to come here and make a fool of me?!" Her melodious voice cracked into a discordant squawk.

Neera looked doubtful, yet she eyed the calico cat carefully. Mazel considered it a huge win that the cantankerous bird wasn't immediately siding with her religious superior. Neera must have really warmed to her. There was hope yet for a friendship between them.

"I think you'd better leave," the Vee said, before Mazel could figure out how to address her bizarre accusation. "My fledgling, please take your visitors back down and away from my temple."

"Thank you for your hospitality," Captain Bataille said without the slightest trace of irony. Only a dog can be so sincerely grateful while getting kicked out on his tail.

Mazel admired that about him, and she knew better than to try sounding half as sincere with her barbed feline tongue. Instead, she slipped her antique scanner back into her pocket, loaded with precious data, and clasped her paws demurely behind her back.

Captain Bataille led the way back down the many flights of winding stairs, stepping slowly and carefully. Mazel followed him, watching his tail droop listlessly before her, brushy fur ruffled by the wind. Behind her, Neera followed in silence. Mazel couldn't tell if it was an angry silence or a sad one. Either way, Mazel figured it wasn't good.

When they reached the ground level courtyard, Captain Bataille asked Neera to find Lt. Unari. He and Mazel would ready the boat for rowing away.

CHAPTER 5
THE POWER OF VISIONS

Once Mazel and the captain were alone on the sandy shore beside the Temple of Yunib, the German Shepherd climbed into the rowboat, sat down, and stared up at the sky. "What does it mean, Big Dog?" he asked. "Am I a messiah in a religion I'd never heard of until three weeks ago? What would that even mean?"

Mazel sat down on the wooden plank seat beside Bataille. Her head only came to his shoulder. His physical presence, now that he was so much larger than her, had a comforting, anchoring quality that she didn't remember when she'd been Darius.

Mazel had a lot of thoughts on the subject of what it meant to be a god in a religion she didn't quite believe in. But she wasn't sure how many of them to share with her friend. She wanted to ease his burden, not drive a wedge between them. It was already surprising that their friendship had survived the last year of upheaval in her life with so little changed.

"Maybe this will all go away if I ignore it," Bataille said. "Focus on the job, and don't worry about the local beliefs."

"I don't think it's going to go away," Mazel said. "From

what I've read of the Avioran beliefs regarding Twig visions..." She drew a deep breath. "If Neera hadn't been there, then maybe it would all go away."

"Why does Commander Neera's presence matter?" Bataille asked, looking down from the sky to focus on Mazel.

"Descriptions of every Broken Twig vision are recorded and shared among all of the Vees on Avia—they're seen as sacred wisdom shared from the gods." And yet, the Vees carefully curated every Broken Twig visitation, creating a false sense of scarcity, apparently to make the visions more valuable. Although, if the visions truly were words from their gods, then Mazel wasn't sure why they needed to be made *more* valuable.

"What if the vision... reveals something personal?" Bataille was clearly thinking about all of the people he'd seen in his vision, all of the people who'd died, all of the people he'd lost. "What if it's something too personal to share?"

Mazel shrugged. "I'm not an expert. I'm just a fast reader, and I spent a day reading up on the Sky Nest and Broken Twigs. Maybe they write down a vague description? I mean, it's not like you gave the Vee very many details to work with. But you did say that you'd been called the Apex. And you said it in front of Neera. I don't think Vee Wya can afford to leave that out of her record, and that means she can't simply disappear what happened here."

"No wonder she was angry," Bataille said. "She doesn't want to believe I'm this mythical figure that she believes in... but the rest of her religious order might. And she won't be able to stand against them if enough of them do." He shook his head. "So what do I do? Renounce my words? Tell them I don't want to be the Apex? I don't even know what the Apex really is!"

"I don't think it's up to you," Mazel said. "The Aviorans will believe what they believe. All you can do is be the best Tri-Galactic Union delegate that you know how to be." Mazel knew that her own advice rang somewhat hollow when she told it to herself, but perhaps it meant more coming from someone else. Regardless, it was the best advice she had to give.

Bataille grinned wolfishly, apparently comforted. "Yeah, I know how to do that." His grin wavered when he caught sight of Commander Neera and Lt. Unari approaching.

The black cat's arms were full of leafy cuttings, piled high in a flat, shallow box. The bird looked dazed, wings folded tightly behind her, and tail feathers splayed widely. Her eyes locked onto the captain, but she said nothing, staying uncharacteristically quiet, as she climbed into the boat and took an oar between her wings.

Unari set her box of cuttings under the plank seat and joined the others. She spent the boat ride back excitedly discussing everything she had learned about the bonsai trees, how they had been gathered and cultivated from every continent on Avia, and their individual botanical histories. She seemed unconcerned by the others' silence as they rowed across the lake. Mazel tried to engage with her. Unlike the black cat, Mazel was not a botanist, but she had been one in past lives.

During the shuttle flight back up to Nexus Nine Base, Unari told them everything she had learned from Isstis about the difficulties faced by Reptassan-Avioran hybrids. The occupation had lasted long enough that there were hybrids of all ages, some of them second or third generation.

Many of the hybrids had turned to the Temples of the Unhatched for shelter and livelihoods. By and large, they were not well-accepted on Avia, but most of them—from what Isstis had told Unari—felt they were better off among the Aviorans than the Reptassans. Especially the ones who couldn't or didn't want to undergo cosmetic surgery to look like full-blooded Reptassans. Artificial scales, apparently, were far easier to construct than functional, believable artificial feathers. Yet, very few of the hybrids wanted to give up whatever natural feathers they had in order to pass for being fully reptilian.

"Feathers are blessing from the Unhatched," Neera muttered, mostly ignoring Unari and focusing on piloting the shuttle. She'd had surprisingly little to say regarding the Avioran-Reptassan hybrids as Unari had talked about them. She wasn't usually a bird who held back her opinions.

"Perhaps the Tri-Galactic Union should offer some scholarships specifically to Avioran-Reptassan individuals to encourage them to join the naval academy," Captain Bataille said. "The Tri-Galactic Union might be a more comfortable place for them than either Avia or Reptiss."

The captain's words turned Neera's head. She looked away from the shuttle's main view screen, where Nexus Nine Base loomed before them like a child's toy, discarded on the endless black sand beach of the sky. The space station was constructed entirely from interconnected hexagons and triangles, pointy and angular and complicated.

Neera stared piercingly at Captain Bataille, taking his measure without saying a word. Finally, she looked back at the main view screen and brought the shuttle in to dock at the corner of one of the hexagons.

Mazel was curious how the tension between Neera and Bataille would play out, but fundamentally, it was not her problem. And the data stored in her antique scanner called to her like a homing beacon. She was so close, possibly so close, to learning where she had truly come from.

As they exited the docked shuttle craft, Mazel asked Lt. Unari, "Do you have lab space for studying those plant samples?"

"Oh, yes," the black cat said amiably. "They've set me up with a corner of the medical bay."

"A corner?" Mazel asked, wondering if she should offer to

share some of her own lab space. Not that botany and physics equipment had all that much overlap.

"The medical bay is huge," Unari said. "Have you seen it? I mean, I do have that squirrel doctor rushing over all the time to chatter at me, but he's had some surprisingly interesting insights for a medical doctor."

"So, the station had no research labs but an extensive medical bay?" Mazel asked. As she said the words, the pieces fell together.

Neera squawked, "The Viper's Perch was where Reptassans shipped any of their officers from the planet who we managed to seriously injure but not quite kill. They'd patch 'em up, and send them back to stand on our wings. If we were injured though? They'd just let us bleed."

Mazel smiled weakly, not knowing how else to respond. Neera's assertion confirmed her suspicions.

This whole space station felt haunted by its violent, horrible past. Its very physical structure had been determined by priorities and plans that centered on the subjugation and destruction of an entire people. Mazel felt sick being there. But she wanted to find her own history, and somehow, it was tangled up—by way of Nexus Nine—with the Aviorans.

As Mazel walked the halls of Nexus Nine Base, heading towards her ramshackle laboratory, she thought about how the history of uplifted cats and dogs on Earth was filled with violence and oppression too.

Dogs had tried to keep cats from space travel. They'd locked cats up for possession of catnip, which was a harmless, recreational drug, and thrown away the keys. Dogs had bullied cats, beaten cats, ignored cats, jailed cats, and at times, shot cats down in the street. Cats had fought hard to attain and defend their rights.

But Mazel was used to those forms of violence and oppression as part of a history book—it was easy to believe they were all in the distant past when she looked at how far the Tri-Galactic Union had come. Over lifetimes, Mazel had become used to tuning out the historical structures that still meant she had to fight harder to be heard as a cat than she had when she was a dog. (And she couldn't imagine how much harder it must be for Dr. Jardine—squirrels had always had it worse in dog-run societies than cats did.)

But that was background noise. She tuned it out and went on with her life, as much as possible.

The history of violence and oppression on Nexus Nine Base—the Viper's Perch—felt so raw and fresh; it chafed at Mazel, leaving her uncomfortable in her own fur, wishing she could be anywhere else, but knowing there was nowhere else she could be that would make the violence that had happened here untrue. Just less salient. And that made her feel guilty for even wanting to escape it.

If there was violence in the universe, why should she be free from seeing it?

But also: how would her observing it... help?

Mazel found the doors to her science lab, and when they slid open, she felt relief soak through her like warm sunlight on a winter day. Wizard O'Neill had installed every piece of equipment. The cot was gone, but the double room actually looked like a science lab. Small and cramped, but a real labo-ratory. Here was a place that Mazel understood, a place where she felt safe and knew what to do.

Mazel plugged her antique scanner into one of the computer consoles and began downloading the data. While it downloaded, she set up a search of the computer's records of Avioran scripture, looking for anything and everything about the Apex. She wanted to be able to support the captain—her dear friend—better, but she could also see the potential for his vision interfering in her research.

If the Aviorans decided that the Tri-Galactic Union shouldn't study the home of their gods, it could become quite difficult to proceed. If at all possible, Mazel wanted to find a way to keep the Avioran religion from interfering in her scientific research. And so far, it had proved invaluable to be able to quote Avioran scripture back to the birds who believed in it.

The computer chimed discordantly, announcing that it had finished downloading the scanner's data. It spoke in an atonally raspy, hissing voice: "Resultssss ssshow the pattern isss a matsch."

Mazel's heart leapt, and she looked the data over herself. It was true. The subatomic distortion pattern from the Broken Twig of Foresight matched the subatomic distortion on her own Rheun chip perfectly.

Lifetimes ago, she had passed through Nexus Nine. Her origins lay on the other side. She was closer to her galaxy of origin than she had been since coming to Earth as an octopus in her distant memories.

Mazel wondered if the species who had created her Rheun half still existed and flourished on the other side of Nexus Nine. Was there a whole civilization of octopuses, enhanced by memory chips, waiting for her in the galaxy on the other side? The Ennea galaxy. She was from the Ennea galaxy.

If there was a whole civilization of enhanced octopuses waiting for her, would they understand her bizarre, patchy history of passing her chip from species to species? Or would they be ethnic purists, keeping their chips strictly inside octopus bodies? Would she be an outcast? Still not understood...

But perhaps, on the other side of Nexus Nine, she would find a whole society full of people who understood what it was like to pass their consciousness from one life to the next, existing in a state of seeming immortality. The idea took her breath away, but it also gave her oxygen, saturating her body with a sustenance she hadn't known she'd been missing. She could hardly wait to board a shuttle and return through Nexus Nine.

Going home, Mazel thought. For once, those words had a meaning deeper than returning to a kittenhood residence where she'd spent the smallest fraction of her life.

The first step was to send an un-crewed probe through the nexus, to make sure it was safe. Of course it was safe. Mazel knew it was safe. Her earlier memory involved travelling through it... But it was better—it was scientific—to be sure, to double check.

There was always the possibility—unlikely though she thought it might be—that the nexus had grown structurally unstable over the centuries. In fact, Mazel realized with real concern, that the Broken Twigs might represent a form of instability that she hadn't seen in the other eight nexuses scattered across the three galaxies.

Mazel felt a chill that had nothing to do with temperature.

Nexus Nine Base was always plenty toasty for furry mammals, having been designed for cold-blooded reptiles. Mazel wished that Lt. O'Neill would apply some of his wizardry to that problem. Though she imagined it was low on the list of priorities compared to broken synthesizers and temperamental elevators.

Before heading to the station's command center to look into dispatching a probe through the nexus, Mazel grabbed a quick lunch at Scharm's Bar. She would have just synthesized something simple in the lab, but every possible outlet that could provide power had been plugged into one of the power-hungry pieces of equipment. Better to have hungry scientists than hungry lab equipment.

If Mazel had eaten alone in the lab, she would have missed out on a game of Chanster's Claws with Quincy and Dr. Jardine. Both the bulgy-eyed amphibioid and the bright-eyed squirrel flirted with her mercilessly, and the calico cat found the distraction pleasant.

They both seemed so young and naive to her, especially the way that they seemed to assume that she was young and naive. There was nothing more naive in Rheun's presence than assuming that the surface was indicative of the depth inside. Mazel Rheun was a well of almost unimaginable depth for creatures who lived a single lifetime.

Mazel had never played Chanster's Claws before, but her Rheun chip was exceptionally good at calculating probabilities, and she had lifetimes of experience with reading other peoples' body language. So she was quite surprised when Dr. Jardine won every round, bushy tail flipping excitedly behind him in his chair. The eager squirrel must be very bright, she thought. She'd have to take him up on his offer—enthusiastic request—that they have dinner together some time.

Belly full and brain rested, Mazel arrived in the three-tiered command center, ready to start work on programming an un-crewed probe. Her station on the lowest ring was in working order today, and she would need it. While most of her research required a laboratory space with dedicated computers, the programming for an un-crewed probe needed to be done on the station's main computer system, in order to interface with all of the station's command systems for remotely communicating with the probe.

Mazel was amazed that Lt. O'Neill had managed to both set up her laboratory and fix her station on the command deck in so little time. She would have to find Lt. O'Neill and thank him for all of his hard work, perhaps synthesize a nice rawhide for him as a thank you gift. She'd loved those when she was a dog.

As Mazel coded a program that would allow the probe to navigate the hyperspatial fluctuations inside of the nexus and scan the far side for as much information as possible, she found herself frequently distracted by the presence of the captain and commander within view on the highest tier.

Captain Bataille had his tennis ball in one paw, and he kept throwing it, catching it, fidgeting with it in the way Mazel knew he did when nervous about an impending dangerous mission. Neera couldn't keep her eyes off of the captain—she'd be deeply engrossed in the work on her console for a few moments at a time, but then her gaze would drift away into the mid-distance, seemingly lost in her own thoughts, and inevitably, her gaze would turn back toward the captain.

The German Shepherd was clearly aware of the bird's distraction and grimaced every time he caught her watching him.

It is not easy working with someone who thinks you're a god. Mazel couldn't even imagine how hard it must be from the other side—working with someone whom you genuinely believe to be a god. Mazel felt deeply for both Shep and Neera.

The balance between Shep and Neera shifted over the next several days as rumors of the captain's vision grew. Whispered birdsong lilted through the command deck, and every Avioran officer took to glancing at Shep, distractedly, while they worked. Shep himself grew more and more irritable.

Mazel was sorely tempted to tell the captain about her own experiences with First Racer dogs treating her weirdly when they knew about her past lives as a human. But a secret told cannot be untold, and there was still a chance that the captain's vision would blow over. Worse, there was a chance that even if Mazel shared her secret, the captain wouldn't find any solace in it—he'd become weird toward her, and there would be no new sense of communion between them. He might consider their experiences too different to learn from her. After all, the captain knew that his gods had existed—the First Race most definitely had walked the Earth and uplifted other mammals to follow in their footprints.

The older Mazel got, the less she understood the very idea of godhood. Why did so many people feel the need to deify and worship? Certainly it could be lonely walking through life, knowing there were no paws guiding your way, but

Mazel couldn't imagine finding comfort in an imaginary presence, too distant to see or feel directly. Only to be inferred.

Although, Mazel did have lifetimes of memories, so many voices, echoing in her head. She didn't travel through life as alone as most creatures did. She had her past to comfort her, and a much longer future to look forward to.

Perhaps, without the Rheun chip, believing in gods was the only way to combat the frightening lack of history to call on when making choices and the terrifyingly limited future with which to enjoy the fruits of those choices.

Guessing in the dark, reaping one reward—one lifetime, however it might turn out—and then disappearing, losing the light of yourself in the eternal darkness of oblivion.

For not the first time, Mazel wondered whether the Rheun chip could be copied, built in bulk, and disseminated across the Tri-Galactic Union. Others could benefit from living more than one life at a time. And yet, she knew from experience, many people were deeply troubled by the idea of sharing their consciousness with people from the past who they hadn't known. Hers was not an immortality that everyone wanted.

She had to admit, the transition from Mazel Tabbith to Mazel Rheun had been rough. It still was... Only a few days before, she had stood on the command deck, quivering, terrified that her most recent oldest friend would reject her.

But every lifetime is filled with fears, both fleeting and lasting.

So many of Mazel's questions would be answered if she could only find the society she had come from. They would have thought these questions through on a societal level with many different minds, bouncing ideas off of each other. Instead of one individual, in isolation, thinking quietly to herself over centuries.

Coding the AI for the un-crewed probe took Mazel most of a week, cobbling together pieces of code from previous probes and accounting for Nexus Nine's differences. During that time, she enjoyed several more games of Chanster's Claws where Dr. Jardine played surprisingly well, met the Tri-Galactic Navy security chief for the station—a large, brown bear named Grawf who wore a chainmail sash over her standard issue uniform—and spent a lot of time listening quietly to the captain as he vented about the difficulty of leading a flock of birds flirting with the idea of worshipping him.

Most of a week was approximately the same amount of time that it took for the Council of Vees to announce an official statement regarding Captain Bataille's vision: they withheld judgment, pending an interview with the captain.

Furious, Captain Bataille paced the halls with Mazel, bouncing his yellow-green tennis ball off the walls as they walked. "Should I do it?" he asked, over and over again.

Mazel's answer didn't seem to make much difference. No matter which answer she tried, he'd just bounce the ball violently off the wall, catch it a few paces farther down the hallway, and ask, "But should I do it, Big Dog? I just don't know! Should I? Should I let them interview me?"

Finally Mazel tired of chasing her friend through the halls, listening to him agonize.

"The Tri-Galactic Union won't care what you do, as long as the work here continues," Mazel snapped, this time refusing to follow the much larger dog, pumping her legs twice as fast as he strode with his.

Captain Bataille paused in his pacing and turned to look at the little calico cat, fur fluffed out from the stress of confronting her old friend and superior officer.

"So tell them you need more time, and keep doing the work." She added, self-interestedly, "You can start by authorizing my project to send an un-crewed probe through the nexus."

Bataille tilted his head and smiled. "That's your work." He

saw right through her self-interest. "Mine is conducting the peoples of Avia into joining the Tri-Galactic Union."

"And if they are to join the TGU, then they'll need to authorize scientific studies regarding the hyperspatial highway that they live next to." Mazel's tail lashed. She was too close to the Ennea galaxy to be held back by a bit of backward religious confusion.

"True," Bataille agreed. "But what if it blows up somehow, all tangled up with this Apex business?"

Mazel had read as much of the scripture about the Apex as she could stomach, but she hadn't found it very useful. The pretty prose and poetic parables had been pleasant enough at first, but they'd grown repetitive and hard to swallow, like too many sugary treats that sour on your tongue and bloat in your stomach. All sugar, no nutrition.

"I wish I could help you," Mazel said. "But the scripture about the Apex is as vague and useless as..." She hesitated, barely catching herself before comparing Avioran scripture to First Racer scripture. She didn't need to open that can of worms. "I don't know. But honestly, based on what I read, you might be the Apex. Some of the similarities, some of the choice of language is uncanny. Maybe you were destined to come here. Maybe some of the Broken Twigs are actually rips in space time, and Avioran scripture is based on true visions of the future."

Mazel wasn't sure she believed any of that, but she couldn't deny that Avioran scripture was surprisingly dodgy about referring to the Apex having actual physical wings. That alone was intriguing. On top of that, the Apex was frequently described as an outsider, a visitor, a traveler, and even the leader of a union. Nonetheless, she had her doubts that exposing oneself to a rip in space-time could lead to hallucinated visions that accurately foretold the future.

Even if the Broken Twigs were stitches in the fabric of space-time that occasionally connected the present to the future—in the same universe, a huge assumption given the infinite infinities of the multi-verse—then it would be shocking if an organic brain could make the slightest sense of that future from the barest glimpse offered through exposure to a Twig.

Although, Mazel realized, she didn't have a wholly organic brain. Her brain was bimodal—organic and Rheun chip. Her Rheun chip would have had a much better chance of properly interpreting data from another point in space-time filtered through a broken, ragged-edged rip.

So why had she been the only person in recorded history to face a Broken Twig and not experience a vision? Mazel had checked the Avioran records thoroughly. Even sub-sentient animals when exposed to the Broken Twigs exhibited all the signs of having experienced a vision. She was the only being who hadn't.

"I've got it!" Mazel exclaimed.

Captain Bataille blinked at her, passed his tennis ball from one paw to the other, and said, "You've got what?"

"Why I didn't experience a vision!" The small calico cat rushed away from the much taller German Shepherd, but he followed after her. She heard his footsteps behind her as she hurried through the halls to her improvised laboratory.

As soon as she arrived, Mazel turned on the most powerful scanner and scanned her own head. "There it is," she said to the captain who had followed her inside.

"Your Rheun chip?" he asked, looking at the scan of her brain that appeared on one of the screens. Most of her brain lit up in bright colors, but the Rheun chip appeared as a spot of shining white, too bright for a single color.

"I didn't experience a vision, because the Rheun chip buffered it, firewalling my brain, essentially." She typed at the console, running processing software over the buffered memories. She knew they must be from her experience with the Broken Twig of Foresight, because there hadn't been any buffered memories only a few weeks ago when she underwent a full medical examination before switching assignments. Nothing else had happened in the last few weeks that would have led to a buffered memory.

In fact, Mazel couldn't remember any time in her long history when the Rheun chip had buffered a memory to protect her from it. This experience was new and unique. That was exciting and also a little frightening.

"I've run the buffered memory through some software that should be able to reinterpret it into a video..." She leaned back from the console, a little afraid to proceed. "Should... I watch it?" She wondered if she should send the captain away. But it was probably too late now. He knew about the buffered vision. She couldn't keep it a complete secret. And honestly, she was a little afraid to watch it alone.

"Alright," Layafette said, placing a heavy paw on her shoulder. "Let's watch it together."

"What if it gets... personal?" Mazel's voice squeaked, more like a mouse than a cat.

Bataille took one of her small paws in his big one. "You just squeeze my paw, and I'll look away, okay?"

Mazel nodded, and she started the video.

Scattered colors appeared across the screen, like infrared vision, fuzzy, pixelated, and unclear. Figures with vague shapes but no clear details moved—several bodies, one crossing a room, and another rocking in a chair. They seemed mammalian and bipedal in shape, but that was about all Mazel could make out.

"Is there any sound?" Bataille asked. "And... can you make it any clearer?"

"I'm not sure." Mazel put her paws back to the keyboard. She tried a few keystrokes, and then the vision came into sharper focus, and a murmuring sound began.

Now she could see that the figure who'd moved across the room was Darius; the figure rocking herself was Augrula.

Other hosts of the Rheun chip—Mazel's previous lives—stood around the room, leaning over consoles, working on computers, farther in the background. Some of them spoke, but none of their words were clear. All of them seemed to be aboard the shuttle Mazel remembered from her earliest memory; the distorted sky of the inside of Nexus Nine flickered by outside the shuttle.

"There are humans in your vision," Bataille said, wonder filling his voice. The sound of his reverence made Mazel shiver, fur fluffing out everywhere that her uniform didn't tamp it down. "Also... octopuses? And what's that outside the shuttle?"

Mazel wasn't sure, but as they continued to watch the shuttle craft distorted as though she was looking at it through a fisheye lens. The insides flipped out, and the outside flipped in. All of her previous selves seemed fine, completely unconcerned even, that their shuttlecraft was now shaped like an M.C. Escher painting. Their background murmurings grew more insistent, and Mazel realized she recognized what they were saying—"Home, come home, almost home." Repeated over and over in a language too ancient for Shep to understand them.

The rippling colors of Nexus Nine flowing through and around the shuttle looked like a river—no, more like a painting of a river. The blue waters were far more colorful, in far brighter and more varying shades, than the actual blue of a river. Among the caricatures of waves and eddies, tentacles appeared. Pearlescent arms with perfectly round sucker discs, twisting around whirlpools in the river and swirling around the inside-out shuttlecraft. Then the vision ended.

"I saw something like that—those strings of pearls," Bataille said.

Mazel blinked, trying to understand what he meant. Did he think the tentacles were strings of pearls?

"Those glowing white strands of circles—I saw those," he insisted.

"In your vision?" Mazel asked.

"Yes, they were everywhere, all around. I thought... I thought they were clouds in the sky." He put his big head in his big paws, ears tilting backward. "It all happened so fast, and I never got to talk about the details... because all the Vee or Neera cared about was the word Apex."

Mazel wondered how many others had seen those same tentacles in their visions and misinterpreted them as strange clouds or strings of pearls. She might need to read more Avioran scripture after all. "Maybe you should talk to the council of Vees," she said. "They might help you interpret your vision. Instead of worrying that they'll judge you or make a decision that you don't like... maybe just tell them your vision to find out what they think about it. They do have more experience with Broken Twig visions than either of us."

Bataille nodded and chewed on his lower lip, showing his sharp canines. "Big Dog," he said, "who were those humans in your vision? Did you... know them?"

Inside of herself, Mazel jumped at the chance to say, "I was them!" But she held her tongue still, trapped behind her own sharp teeth. She kept her mouth shut and only shook her head, ears flattened as far back as they would go.

"I'm sorry," he said. "If you don't want to talk about it..."

"I don't." But she could tell that wouldn't stop him from speculating. Perhaps speculating was better than knowing.

Captain Bataille stared levelly at Mazel for some time. Finally he nodded and said, "All right. I'll meet with the Council of Vees. And you can launch your probe."

"Thank you!" Mazel squeezed the captain's paw hard, realizing she was still holding it. "But... just one thing... can we launch the probe before you speak with the Council of Vees?"

The captain shrugged. "I don't see why not. As you say,

the Aviorans won't make much headway with joining the Tri-Galactic Union if they try to block important scientific research in their sector, and as far as I've been told, they are still serious about joining the Tri-Galactic Union, regardless of--" He shook a paw dismissively, perhaps a little disgustedly, at the computer screen where Mazel's vision had played out. The vision was over now, and the screen had frozen on an image of Darius. "--all of this vision nonsense."

"I'm sure the Vees will *love* that attitude." Mazel's muzzle quirked into a taunting, teasing, lopsided grin.

"You know what I mean," Bataille said.

"I do," Mazel agreed, wishing that Bataille understood that his attitude toward the Avioran religion and her attitude towards the religion of the First Racers wasn't all that different. But she was still too scared to tell him.

CHAPTER 6
DISCOVERING A NEW GALAXY

The command deck was crowded—seemingly full of every Avioran officer onboard Nexus Nine Base, every Tri-Galactic Navy scientist, and of course, Omoleura—when Mazel launched the un-crewed probe toward Nexus Nine. The anticipation was palpable.

Aviorans whispered about the Apex and the Sky Nest—many of them seemed to believe they would soon be hearing the voice of their gods, the wisdom of the Unhatched, sent through the scientific scanners of the probe. The Tri-Galactic Navy scientists whispered less; their excitement was more straightforward and less fraught—they would learn something interesting today, regardless of what exactly the probe discovered, new knowledge is new knowledge. They had fewer hopes to be dashed and thus could wear their excitement on their sleeves, where the Aviorans had to cradle their sacred, delicate hopes like fledgling babes with untested wings, unsure yet of whether they'd ever fly.

Omoleura stood beside Mazel as they watched the explosion of colors on the central holo-viewscreen that happened as the probe entered Nexus Nine. Today, Omoleura looked—vaguely—like a bird again. As much as zhe ever did.

Complex wings folded behind zim, Omoleura strutted back and forth, impatiently. Mazel could understand the feeling. After the explosion of colors, Nexus Nine went dark again. They wouldn't hear from the shuttle until after it had reached the other side, scanned the area, turned around, and returned through the nexus. Any signals the probe sent from the far side of the nexus would take—possibly—millions of years to return to Nexus Nine Base directly, depending on how far away the galaxy Ennea was.

Of course, if the probe didn't survive the trip through the nexus or met an inhospitable environment on the other side, it might never return. Mazel forced herself to breath regularly, as much as she could. She kept catching herself holding her breath, but it would do no good to hold her breath waiting for the probe if it never returned.

After an interminable passage of time—twenty minutes that felt longer than some of Rheun's entire lifetimes—the colorful lines of Nexus Nine exploded like fireworks on the central holo-screen again. And data began to pour into Mazel's console, transmitted to the station by the probe.

The room erupted in cheers—whistling, tweeting, barking, meowing, even the doctor's excited voice chittering, "I knew it would work! I just knew it!"

Omoleura leaned close to Mazel and said with zir cello-like voice, "What do the readings show? Can we go there?"

Mazel examined the data from every angle as quickly as she could, and it all came out the same: "Yes, the galaxy on the other side of Nexus Nine is a spiral galaxy, and not one we've encountered before. The nexus seems to open near the middle of one of the spiral arms—well within range of a variety of star systems with habitable planets."

As Mazel spoke, the command deck fell silent, everyone listening closely to her quiet voice.

"Captain, I request permission to identify this newly discovered galaxy with the moniker Ennea, as it lies on the other side of the ninth nexus discovered by the Tri-Galactic Union." The question was largely ceremonial, as the name had already been in informal use in scientific circles for some weeks now. However, Mazel thrilled at the chance to officially name an entire galaxy.

"Permission granted, Lieutenant." The captain's wolfish muzzle split in a huge grin; he looked happier than he had all week. There's nothing quite like discovering an entirely new galaxy, ripe for exploration, to galvanize even the most weary of spirits.

"How soon can we send a crewed mission through the Sky Nest?" Omoleura asked, complex wings buzzing.

Mazel had been tempted to ask the same question, but she was glad it came from someone who could unflinchingly refer to Nexus Nine as the Sky Nest. The captain was more likely to authorize a crewed mission if he felt like it wouldn't risk upsetting the Aviorans.

"Soon," the captain said, tossing his tennis ball from one paw to the other. "Start making plans, Lieutenant Rheun. Assemble a team and be ready."

Mazel's team assembled themselves for her.

Omoleura was already beside her, vibrating with excitement at the idea of going back to the galaxy zhe believed zhe'd originally come from.

Neera hopped her way down from the highest level of the command deck to insist that the Avioran people be represented on the first mission through the Sky Nest, and then to offer herself as an appropriate representative with both diplomatic and battle training. Mazel had no doubts that Neera had battle training; she had a harder time believing that the bird had the necessary self-restraint and delicacy to ever function as a diplomat. Though it was possible that she had endured some sort of diplomatic training. Mazel did not envy the instructor who'd had to teach her.

Next Lt. Unari worked her way through the crowd on the

lowest ring of the command deck from where she'd watched the probe's return beside her husband, the wizard O'Neill. The black cat explained with gleams in her green eyes that her expertise in biology would be invaluable when encountering previously undiscovered species of both plant and animal life. "I requested this post for exactly these kinds of opportunities," she said.

Lt. O'Neill had worked his way through the crowd behind her and affirmed, "She did. She requested this post without consulting or even telling me. That's how excited she was about it. And now I'm here patching together broken Reptassan computer systems!"

"And we're so glad that you are," Neera said with an uncharacteristic warmth. The West Highland Terrier was so invaluable as an engineer that even a cranky bird like Neera had already come around and felt grateful to have him here.

O'Neill harrumphed and grumbled, "Well, I guess I do like the challenge." He backed away, glancing around like he would be more comfortable if he had a broken piece of technology in his paws to be fixing. "Just don't get lost in that faraway galaxy—I expect my beloved to return to me and not leave me wandering the over-heated halls of this wretched space station like a ghost on the Scottish moor."

"You'd make a good imitation of a ghost with that white fur," Mazel offered. She could say that, because she had mostly white fur too.

O'Neill scowled beneath his beard.

"Don't worry so much," Lt. Unari said. "Except, you know, about keeping the station running while we're gone."

The black cat touched her pink nose gently to the white dog's larger black one. Nose to nose. Then Lt. O'Neil shuffled away, muttering about synthesizers that wouldn't synthesize anything but marshmallow fluff.

The final member of the team to introduce herself was Grawf—the large, brown-furred Ursine security officer whom

Omoleura didn't want to share zir station with, who was apparently a certified expert on diplomacy.

"You must be kidding!" Omoleura squealed like a violin being tuned. "You want to work with me on securing this station, but you don't want to do the ONE thing that would actually be useful to me? Standing in for me when I have to be away?" Omoleura's complicated wings rearranged themselves, distorting zir bird-like appearance, and then zhe chuckled sourly like a violin being kicked across the floor. "From two security chiefs down to none. That sure makes sense."

"Chief Omoleura," the bear rumbled, adjusting the pewter-colored chainmail sash that lay over her uniform, "if you would actually coordinate with me on a day-to-day basis, you'd understand that the Tri-Galactic Navy chain of command means the station is more than sufficiently protected. I've arranged for multiple redundancies at every level. So Nexus Nine Base won't suffer at all if both of us go on the mission through the nexus."

"Your problem," Omoleura sighed like a dying violin, "is that you don't understand how I do things. I have a very particular way of doing things."

"And your problem," Grawf retorted amiably in her deep, rumbly voice, "is that you don't delegate."

Neera squawked in laughter. "The bear's got you there," she said, bumping Omoleura with a wing. The insect rearranged all of zir complicated limbs in response, visibly relaxing at the bird's touch.

"Very well," Omoleura conceded with a soft chirp like a newly restrung violin being gently plucked to test its tuning.

Each member of Mazel's team—black cat, bird, unique insect, and bear—turned to look expectantly at the calico cat in charge of them. "Well," she said, "we're going to wipe out Captain Bataille's array of senior officers... but I guess we have a team."

"Not quite," Captain Layayette interjected, approaching the group.

The crowd of onlookers on the station had mostly dispersed, leaving only the usual officers at their usual posts. However, the captain had Quincy, the frog-like Phiboon, standing beside him.

"I would also like to join you on the inaugural visit to Galaxy Ennea," Quincy galumphed, neck swelling and shrinking as he spoke. "Beautiful name, by the way! Ennea. I love it. Love it."

Mazel blinked at the froggy alien. Since she'd arrived on the station, all she'd heard about him was shade, and all of his dealings had seemed shady enough to warrant it. He ran a black market and gambled in Scharm's Bar all day long.

"Why do you want to come?" Mazel asked, aghast. What she really wanted to know was why the captain was standing beside the Phiboon; why he had brought the Phiboon to her. Was the captain supporting this black market dealer's request to join her on a scientific—and possibly diplomatic—mission?

Mazel couldn't imagine what use Quincy could be in analyzing data gathered from uninhabited worlds. And the froggy alien seemed more likely to be a liability than an asset if they did encounter any sentient lifeforms. Mazel would hardly like this frog to be another civilization's first impression of life in the triple galaxies.

Quincy didn't answer Mazel's question, instead turning his wide, bulging eyes up toward the captain. The German Shepherd cleared his throat and said, "Apparently, Quincy applied for and received special envoy status from his people on Phibias, and the Tri-Galactic Union would like us to accommodate his special status by including him on any missions to the newly discovered galaxy that he wants to join."

Mazel skewed one ear, effectively asking her captain—and

old friend who would understand her without the need for actual words—"WHY?"

Quincy galumphed proudly, "Phibias has the largest and fastest replenishing network of power crystal mines that's been discovered anywhere in the three galaxies." His neck swelled like a balloon before shrinking back to size. "The Tri-Galactic Navy wants to keep us happy so that they can keep their ships flying through space at faster than light speeds. That's what you actually wanted to know, isn't it?"

The frog was savvy. Mazel had to give him that. "Okay then," she said. "I guess you're in. That makes a team of six, a perfect complement for a long range shuttle craft. We'll plan on a two-day mission but bring supplies for a week, in case we get caught up in anything particularly interesting."

"You can use *Star-Skipper 1* for the mission," Captain Bataille said. "It should suit your needs."

"Thank you, Captain," Mazel said. *Star-Skipper 1* would feel tight if they stayed in Galaxy Ennea for more than a few days, but its scanners were particularly powerful. Not a lot of crew accommodations—simple bunks in a barracks-style room—but packed to the gills with scientific scanners.

Mazel quickly decided on assignments for her team—checking the shuttle craft, loading it with backup supplies, and uploading the proper programs for scanning, analyzing, categorizing, and mapping newly discovered star systems. Once her team members had dispersed, she said to the captain, "We should be ready to leave by tomorrow morning."

Mazel wanted to get the mission underway as soon as possible. Fortunately, Captain Bataille looked sympathetic to her desire. He nodded at her absently. "Yes, yes, that sounds reasonable. I suppose, I'll get out of your way, Big Dog, and let you prepare."

Mazel worried about how Bataille would fare while she was off galivanting through a new galaxy, but at least she was bringing Commander Neera with her. He'd still have a planet full of deeply religious Aviorans to contend with—but Mazel was taking the most directly contentious one off of his paws.

Mazel spent the rest of the day going through her lab, packing every portable piece of equipment, everything that she could possibly need. As she packed the bag of equipment that would probably never get opened during the trip —*Star-Skipper 1* was plenty well enough equipped without any of the ramshackle equipment from her lab—she kept remembering how the antique scanner in her pocket had saved her from missing out on scanning the Broken Twig of Foresight.

Mazel wanted to be prepared for every possibility. Every scenario. Or perhaps, she was just scared about what she'd find on the other side of Nexus Nine, because the most likely option was that they'd find nothing, nothing at all on their first mission. Yet she couldn't help getting her hopes up anyway. She wondered if Omoleura felt the same.

Once the preparations were done, the rest of Mazel's team decided to get dinner at the Ursine restaurant. She declined to join them, choosing instead to spend a fitful night trying to sleep. She wanted to be well rested for this mission, but too many voices—all of her old selves—spent the night yammering in her head, wondering what she'd find, wondering how she'd feel, wondering, wondering, wondering.

Mostly, Mazel thought she'd feel tired, but she got up earlier than she had to anyway. She checked the news feeds on her computer before leaving her quarters. All of the Avioran news focused entirely on the captain's impending debriefing by the council of Vees. All of the Tri-Galactic Union news was about the galaxy Ennea. All of the eyes of her scientific community were on her, and Mazel felt their weight.

Mazel expected to arrive at the shuttle before any of the rest of her team, but she was surprised to discover Lt. Unari pacing the corridor beside the shuttle's airlock, long black tail twitching beside her.

"Lt. Rheun!" Unari exclaimed. "I came early. I'm just so excited about what we might find today."

"So am I," Mazel said, smiling warmly at the other cat. She felt the smile reach all the way to the tips of her whiskers. It was good to know that she wasn't the only one who was restless with excitement—the prospect of exploring a new galaxy was truly exciting to anyone of a scientific mindset, not just because she had hopes of finding her society of origin. That made her feel better, easier. It reminded her that there were wonders to be found in Ennea, regardless of whether she found exactly what she was looking for.

"Let's get onboard," Mazel said. "Warm the shuttle up for when the others arrive."

The two cats passed through the airlock—it didn't need to be cycled, since the shuttle was pressurized to match the station's atmosphere. Once inside, Mazel was surprised again.

Quincy was draped in an awkward sprawl over the shuttle's main pilot's seat, bulbously-fingered hand covering his head.

"Do you... have a hangover?" Lt. Unari meowed at the Phiboon. She whispered to Mazel, "He was drinking an awful lot of some bubbly green stuff last night."

"Fortunately," Mazel said, "his skills aren't critical to the mission." She raised her voice and said in a commanding tone, "Quincy, get yourself into the barracks and stay out of the way."

"I don't have a hangover," the frog galumphed, but he wobbled as he hopped down the shuttle's one hall toward the small barracks.

Perhaps he didn't have a hangover, Mazel thought, because he was still drunk. Maybe it was for the best. If he spent the whole mission in the barracks, sleeping off his alcoholic stupor, at least it would keep him out of the rest of their paws.

A blood-curdling scream came from the barracks, moments after Quincy hopped into them. The two cats came running and found the frog pointing and jumping and swelling his neck out like a balloon, only to let the air out in more blood-curdling screams. His bulbous fingers were pointing at a green and gold lump, affixed to the ceiling in the corner of the barracks. The lump pulsed softly, like it was breathing, and filaments of it clung to the ceiling like roots or clinging vines. It looked something like a cross between a dirt-covered flower bulb and a blob of mucus.

"What are you shrieking about, water-breather?" squawked a voice from one of the bunks.

Quincy blinked his large eyes and shut his wide mouth in surprise. But he kept pointing urgently at the pulsing glob in the upper corner.

"Haven't you ever seen a chrysalis before?" the voice squawked from the bunk. "Now, hush, we're sleeping in here."

"Neera?" Mazel asked, surprised. "It's morning, actually... Almost time for our departure. Did you sleep here all night?"

"Of course," Neera whistled cheerfully, sounding more like a songbird than Mazel had ever heard her sound before. The bird had built a nest for herself by coiling up the regulation blanket and she was wearing a robe that looked a little like flannel pajamas. She seemed quite cozy. "I came early," she said, almost singing. "I didn't want to be late for..." She didn't have to say anything about the Unhatched for it to be clear that they were on her mind. Instead, she smiled, eyes twinkling. "It's a big day. I wanted to be ready for it."

While they talked, Lt. Unari climbed up on the top bunk closest to the chrysalis. "This is fascinating," she said. "I've never seen a chrysalis quite like this." She reached toward it with a black-furred paw.

"Do you mind?" Neera squawked. "That's Omoleura in there, not some specimen for you to poke at."

"I'm sorry," Lt. Unari said, backing down from the bunk. Once her paws hit the floor, she added, "I wonder if we'll meet more insects like him--"

"Zir," Neera interrupted. "Z pronouns, please."

"Right, sorry again. Like zir in the Ennea galaxy."

"Well, that is why zhe's coming along," Neera squawked. "Now if you'd all get out of here..."

Omoleura's chrysalis began splitting down the middle, and zir fuzzy blue wings showed inside, wet and gleaming. The sight felt far too personal, and Mazel didn't think the security chief had expected an audience for zir emergence.

"Come on," Mazel said, directing Lt. Unari and Quincy back toward the door. "Maybe we can synthesize something for you to eat," she said to the frog, "something to take off the edge of your hangover." Or something to sober him up.

Mazel and Unari prepared the shuttle for take-off while Quincy gobbled up a plate of synthesized scrambled eggs. Eventually, Neera emerged from the barracks, dressed in her usual uniform, and Omoleura followed behind her like a reflection. The insect looked even more like Neera today than zhe had before—zhe was not only mimicking the overall Avioran shape, but also Neera's purple-blue coloring, right down to the ruby tips of her pinion feathers and the splash of red feathers under her throat. Although, the red fuzz under Omoleura's imitation throat was narrower, squeezed between zir multi-faceted eyes.

"Are we all here, then?" Omoleura droned, wryly. "I wasn't expecting a tour through the barracks more than half an hour before the stated departure time."

"I wasn't either," Mazel said. She had expected to be the first one here. "I guess, we're just waiting on Grawf now."

"Ahem," a deep voice rumbled. "I am precisely on time. I

do not keep people waiting." The bear loomed in the open airlock hatch. She filled most of it.

"Please, come inside," Mazel said. "Let's get settled, cycle the hatch, and ask for permission to depart."

The team checked over the equipment on the shuttle one last time. Each of the Tri-Galactic Union officers—Mazel, Unari, and Grawf—had come with nothing but the uniforms on their backs when it came to personal items, trusting the shuttle to be properly equipped to keep them comfortable. But the other three—Neera, Omoleura, and Quincy—had each brought a small overnight bag, which they stashed under their bunks.

Once they were all strapped into their seats, the airlock cycled, and the shuttle was ready to fly. Grawf took the pilot's seat, and Mazel took the command chair beside her. The others were stationed behind them. Mazel opened a communication channel to the command deck and said, "*Star-Skipper 1* is ready to depart. Permission to undock?"

Captain Bataille's face appeared on the shuttle's viewscreen. The German Shepherd was standing on the highest tier of the command deck, and he said, "Permission granted. We will all eagerly await your return."

The view of the command deck disappeared, returning the viewscreen to displaying the dark expanse of star field where Nexus Nine lay waiting like an unlit firework. Or an unhatched egg.

Mazel's fur prickled all over her body, trying to fluff out but restrained by her uniform. Her tail twitched, but she managed to restrain it from full-on swishing. Working to hold her voice steady, she said, "Lieutenant Grawf, please take us out, and set a course through Nexus Nine."

"Aye, Lieutenant," the bear rumbled, sounding very formal.

Mazel appreciated Grawf's professionalism, but she wondered if she should have made a point of joining the team for dinner last night. She'd spent at least a little time with each of the other members of her team, and she felt that she could be easy with them. There was a comfortable give and take in their familiarity. With Grawf, however, there was a stiffness, and Mazel hoped she'd get a chance to fix that.

"How is the colony on Ursa Minuet's second moon coming?" Mazel asked, hoping to thaw the chill between them. "The last time I visited the system, they'd just finished construction on the atmo-bubble, and they were about to begin planting trees. I saw cargo-haulers with whole bays filled with seedlings!"

Grawf glanced sidewise at the little calico cat, looking quite surprised. "Those seedlings are trees taller than the Gragoria Tower now," she rumbled, turning her eyes back to the viewscreen. "You do not look old enough to have seen them as seedlings."

"Looks can be deceiving," Mazel said. She'd have followed up, but instead, her breath was taken away by the sight of the viewscreen exploding with light. Bright lines of red, blue, chartreuse, lemon yellow, candy floss pink, and royal purple flashed, slicing through the darkness and layering over each other in a cacophony of colors.

Then the ship warped around them. Mazel's stomach lurched as her eyes told her that space itself was bulging and bleeding away to the sides, like it had in the tiny, grainy vision she'd watched in her laboratory. On a screen, the effect had looked like a fish-eye lens. In person... it felt like falling off of the edge of the universe. She wished now that the Rheun chip hadn't buffered the vision as it happened, since experiencing the space-time distortion of entering the nexus in a vision might have better prepared her for this feeling like the world was turning inside out around her.

"We've entered the hyperspatial folds of the nexus," Grawf rumbled, her usually deep voice distorted and drawn out until it sounded even deeper.

The bright colors of the entrance to the nexus smoothed and melted into flowing swirls, more like the cartoony river Mazel had seen on the video of her buffered vision. Blues, purples, and touches of yellow danced and twisted on the viewscreen like a painting by the ancient human artist Vincent van Gogh. Starry, starry night, indeed. For an instant that felt like an eternity, Mazel became convinced that Van Gogh must have also carried a neural chip, whispering memories of nexus travels into his brain; he had been a fellow traveler across the centuries, also originating in the galaxy Ennea.

Then Mazel wondered if she, herself, had once been Van Gogh. Vincent van Rheun. She would remember that, wouldn't she? Cutting off her own ear? But then, she remembered the first time that she—as an octopus—chose to pass her neural chip on to a human, and it had been more than a century after the famous painter had died.

Mazel could not have been Van Gogh. And Van Gogh was unlikely to have been a fellow octopus.

Suddenly, Mazel felt a strange, shadowy sensation like she wasn't alone inside her own mind. Arguably, she'd felt that way all year, ever since having the Rheun chip implanted, but this was different. She felt like she wasn't alone, and like she couldn't hear the thoughts of whoever else was with her. She felt separated from... some aspect of herself.

And suddenly, she knew with absolute certainty that she'd felt this sensation before, but the first time she hadn't recognized it: the Rheun chip was buffering another experience. Somehow, the nexus was speaking to her, calling to her, affecting her like the Broken Twig of Foresight had. She was experiencing—but being stopped from experiencing—a vision.

Mazel wanted desperately to know what vision her neural chip self was experiencing, but she didn't think she'd have a chance to find out for some time. She did not want to share her vision—whatever it was—with the rest of her team. For goodness sake, apparently, she didn't even want to share it with herself. And the space aboard the shuttle was small. Everyone in everyone else's space. She would have to wait until they returned to Nexus Nine Base before accessing this new vision.

And that would be a while.

Colors exploded on the viewscreen again, and space blorped back into its proper shape like gelatin plopping out of a complex mold after stretching to cling to the sides as long as possible.

A fresh new galaxy full of different stars in different configurations stretched before *Star-Skipper 1* like a licorice jello dessert shaped like a beautiful castle. Mazel couldn't wait to sink her teeth into it.

"We've emerged in the galaxy Ennea!" Grawf announced. The bear looked genuinely excited. It was about time.

"Alright," Mazel said, "Let's get all of these scanners running, and learn everything we can!"

CHAPTER 7
OFF THE RAILS

fter the initial blush of excitement, several hours of studious, focused concentration and contemplation followed. Numbers streamed over screens—fascinating, mesmerizing numbers—each one representing a star or planet; asteroid field or nebula; likelihood of habitability and—even more exciting—likelihood of already being inhabited.

Mazel was in seventh heaven; her crew was less thrilled. Quincy, Neera, and Omoleura disappeared back into the barracks to play a game of Chanster's Claws. Even Lt. Unari seemed to grow weary of cataloguing star systems by their likelihood of containing biological elements—native plants and animals—that she could study if they went to them... but that were too far away as they floated in space beside the currently invisible nexus just scanning, scanning, scanning.

Grawf was the only officer who seemed to fully understand what she'd signed on for, and she stayed stalwartly at her post, helping Mazel run scans and categorize data without the slightest complaint. The bear seemed to genuinely enjoy the clerical side of doing science.

As they worked, Mazel and Grawf chatted off and on

about the latest politics and news from Ursa Minuet. The bears had extended their civilization outward from their home world to include two settlements on other planets in their system, currently undergoing rapid terraformation, and also a colony world in a neighboring star system.

Of course, there was a great deal of internal political competition for which dynasties could claim the strongest positions in the new settlements. Mazel was happy to hear that her former dynasty—Augrula's dynasty—had claimed a substantial portion of one of the continents on the colony world in the neighboring star system. Mazel couldn't get that kind of news from most Tri-Galactic Union sources, since part of the requirements for joining the TGU involved worldwide peace and cooperation. So, internal strife was kept on the downlow, but that didn't mean competition didn't still happen.

Grawf seemed to enjoy telling the small calico cat about her home world. "Most Tri-Galactic Navy officers aren't interested in Ursa Minuet politics," the bear rumbled appreciatively. She eyed Mazel, probably gauging whether the calico cat was ready to explain the source of her interest.

But the calico cat was not. Mazel was enjoying talking to someone who didn't know her complex history too much to spoil it just yet. Besides, being mysterious comes naturally to cats. Especially calico ones with lopsided markings.

"Let's break for lunch," Mazel said. "While we eat, we can go over our findings and decide on the best course of action from here."

There were so many worlds they could visit. But for this mission, they'd probably have to choose just one. This was, fundamentally, an initial scouting mission after all. More trips would be made later. And yet, Mazel desperately hoped that from the list of planets they'd catalogued—a dry collection of numbers and statistics—she could manage to select the diamond in the rough. A world inhabited by octopi who'd enhanced themselves with neural chips, ready to embrace her with open tentacles.

For lunch, Mazel synthesized herself a sushi roll thick with salty, tangy salmon eggs. She was feeling especially connected to her ancient octopus origins and wanted to eat something appropriate. Fortunately, while Darius had hated fish and fish eggs, Mazel loved them. Just one way that cats and octopuses are more alike than dogs and octopuses.

All six of them ate in the barracks. Quincy kept playing Chanster's Claws with the only one who would join him—Lt. Unari. The black cat hadn't lost any money to him yet and thus hadn't become soured on the game. While each of them munched on their synthesized choices of food—wriggly plates of worms for the bird, mimic-bird, bear, and frog; and a different style of sushi roll for the other cat—they passed around a port-screen showing the statistics regarding the closest hundred or so habitable planets.

"I'm happy with any world likely to have plant life," Unari said, passing the port-screen on to Quincy.

The frog didn't glance at the screen at all before handing it on to Neera. He galumphed, "We should go to whichever star system has the most radio traffic coming from it. Busy civilizations have more goods to trade." He went back to rolling the collection of dice and tokens for his game.

Neera studied the port-screen carefully before telling Mazel, "For whatever reason, the Unhatched chose the Apex, and the Apex sent you on this mission. I trust you'll make the best choice." She tried to hand the port-screen to Omoleura, but the insect quivered all over and shook zir head, unwilling to take it. Instead Neera passed the port-screen to Grawf.

"Do you call the captain that," Mazel said, "to his face?"

"What?" Neera asked. "The Apex? That's what he is."

No wonder Bataille had been stressed out, Mazel thought. "He must love that," she said.

Neera nodded curtly. "He doesn't seem to," she admitted.

"But it's accurate, and I'm far more concerned with what the Unhatched think than with what he thinks."

"Even though the Apex is an instrument of the Unhatched?" Mazel asked, challenging the bird. She knew Avioran scripture pretty well by this point. At least, the parts of it about the Sky Nest, Broken Twigs, and the Apex.

"Why are the Avioran gods called the Unhatched?" Unari asked, laying down her hand of cards. She seemed to have tired of Chanster's Claws even faster than Neera and Omoleura who'd played all morning.

Mazel and Neera exchanged a glance, silently negotiating who would answer Unari's questions. Mazel didn't want to presume, but Neera spread her pinion feathers, gesturing for the calico cat to go ahead. So, Mazel answered, "The Unhatched supposedly--"

Neera coughed, spluttering over Mazel's use of the word "supposedly," but she didn't actually interrupt, so Mazel proceeded.

"--predate the universe itself. Everything in the universe—all of the stars and planets and everything on them hatched from eggs laid by the Unhatched, but the Unhatched themselves have existed since before time or space."

Unari nodded, but the laughter in her green eyes clearly stated that she found the whole thing to be nonsense.

Mazel didn't entirely disagree. She was half glad and half disappointed that Shep wasn't here to make an inappropriate joke about the chicken coming before the egg. Or rather, to smile at her and break into laughter because they both knew what he was carefully NOT saying.

Grawf's deep voice interrupted their theological tangent to say: "I've picked the best star-system—a high concentration of radio signals, several habitable planets, near several other star systems with habitable planets, and not the closest option to our current location."

"Why does that matter?" Unari asked.

"We don't want to reveal the location of the only known passage to our own galaxy," Grawf rumbled. "If at all possible, we want to disguise our origins, in order to protect ourselves from potential hazards."

"Potential hazards," Omoleura crooned in a mocking tone. "You mean hostile civilizations."

"Yes, I do," Grawf agreed. "And it's a danger we should take very seriously." She handed the port-screen back to Mazel. The electronic device looked small cradled in her large brown paws.

Mazel took the port-screen and looked at the star system Grawf had selected. "This looks like a good choice," she agreed. "Whenever you're ready, Lieutenant Grawf, please return to the helm and set a course. It looks like it'll be a three hour flight at a casual speed."

"I could get us there faster," Grawf said, "but it's probably better not to strain the engines if we don't have to."

"Very good," Mazel said.

And the next thing she knew, there was a hard, cold, concrete slab beneath her, slick and wet. Her fur felt moist, sticking against her body, and her shoulder was sore, like she'd been lying on the cold floor for hours.

"Are you okay?" Grawf's voice rumbled, but it was coming from the wrong direction, like the bear had somehow teleported across the room.

Except they weren't in the shuttle craft barracks anymore. They seemed to be in a concrete room—four concrete walls, concrete ceiling, and concrete floor. There were seams in one of the walls, like maybe it was a big, heavy door. The only light came from recessed bulbs hidden behind panels in the ceiling. Mazel pushed herself up from the floor, feeling confused and lost. She felt sure that she'd forgotten something. Had time skipped around her?

"Are you okay, Lieutenant Rheun?" Grawf repeated.

Mazel put a paw to her head. She touched the base of her

own skull, like she was looking for something there. Something missing. Her life felt short. She felt blind. She couldn't see. Well, not literally blind. She could see the dingy, dirty concrete cell around her, and when she turned her head, she saw the big brown bear, Grawf, leaning over her, and she saw a black cat, Lt. Unari, in the corner, paws wrapped around her knees, clutching the tip of her tail and rocking herself.

The chameleoid frog, Quincy, was sprawled on the floor looking dead. Mazel hoped he wasn't dead. His skin was an ashen shade of gray... of course, his coloring matched the concrete floor under him. Then the frog snerrked, snoring like a buzz saw, and a ripple of pinkish-red shivered over his body, perfectly matched by a ripple of pinkish-red in his expensive, perfectly tailored suit. The suit's camouflage abilities were still working, but it looked otherwise tattered and dingy. At least, Mazel knew Quincy was alive.

But... the blindness. She couldn't see her past anymore.

"Who is... Lieutenant Rheun?" Mazel asked.

The large bear helped Mazel up from the floor. Once she had her paws under her, the bear said, "You—you're Lieutenant Rheun."

"Tabbith," she said. "Don't you mean... Oh no." And she knew what she couldn't see. All of her past lives were gone. "What happened?" She could hear the frantic tone in her voice, but she couldn't feel it. She couldn't feel anything now. Just numbness and smallness. Because all of her voices that told her how she felt were gone. Darius... Aug... something... Aurgrooo... Who had come before Darius?

Mazel could remember Darius, because she'd known him in this life. Mazel had known Darius. But she didn't remember who'd come before him. Someone who wasn't a cat... or a dog...

There was no one in her head telling her what to think. She was all alone inside herself. Mazel started to cry, but she was still a Tri-Galactic Navy officer. She swallowed her tears, hiding them as much as she could.

To Mazel's great surprise, Grawf wrapped big bear arms around her and squeezed tight. The calico cat melted into the hug and let the steady pressure calm her. When the bear finally stepped away, releasing her, Mazel said, "Thank you. I needed that."

Grawf nodded solemnly, too proud to talk about the moment of intimacy, but too good of a bear to not offer comfort where comfort was needed. "Now, what do you mean, 'what happened'?"

"The last thing I remember," Mazel said, "was choosing which star system to pursue... We were finishing lunch. You were going to set a course and pilot the ship there when you were ready. Did we get attacked? What happened to the shuttle?"

In the corner of the concrete cell, Unari stopped rocking herself and looked over at Mazel. "That's really the last thing you remember?"

"Yes..." Mazel was suddenly very worried. How much of her life had been taken away from her? Had they been in this cell for months? How had they gotten here? She asked, "Where are Neera and Omoleura?" But she was almost afraid of the answer. Were they dead? Did she want to know? She felt so young and lost.

Mazel remembered being old and wise, but all of her years of wisdom were gone. She cradled one of her paws against the base of the skull, as if her memories were leaking out, and she could stop the mnemonic bleeding by staunching the flow of memories with her paw.

But the memories were already gone. All of her past selves, all of those voices had been like friends inside of her, but they wouldn't talk to her anymore. The chip in her brain wasn't working. Was it broken? Or were the signals connecting her brain to the chip being blocked?

"We don't know what happened to Commander Neera and Chief Omoleura," Unari answered.

"The Carapids separated us from them as soon as they boarded the *Star-Skipper 1*," Grawf rumbled.

"Carapids..." Mazel repeated. The word meant nothing to her, but Grawf had said it like it should. "Some kind of insect?" she asked, but she was having trouble focusing on the here and now. Ironic, since for the first time in a year, she didn't have centuries of memories to distract her from living in the present. And her memories of the last year were... at best... hazy. Like she could only remember half of them.

Grawf and Unari began describing an insectoid race that had attacked and commandeered their shuttle craft, but Mazel could barely hear them over the deafening silence inside her own head.

Why wasn't her neural chip working? She tapped the back of her skull, softly at first but then harder and harder, as if she could joggle a complicated, ancient piece of machinery into working by hitting it hard enough. Her ears flattened, and her whiskers slicked back against her face.

"Where are you?" Mazel muttered to the voices and memories missing from her own mind. But what she really meant was, *"Where am I?"* because she didn't feel like herself anymore with half of her mind gone silent. She hadn't realized how fully she'd managed to integrate the organic and electronic components of herself until the electronic half had gone quiet. She hoped there was nothing wrong with it. She wished she could remember if this had ever happened before...

Unari came across the cell, stepping over the frog sprawled on the floor and still snoring, to get to Mazel. The black cat grabbed the calico cat's orange and white paws with her black ones, prying them away from the back of the cali-co's neck.

There was blood, wet and red, in her crescent claws and

smeared in the fur at the tips of her paws, Mazel noticed once her paws were in front of her, still gripped tightly by Unari's.

"What are you doing?" Unari asked. "Why are you trying to scratch off the back of your head?"

"My..." Mazel couldn't remember the name of the chip. Wait, it had been Darius' last name. *Rheun* chip. It's not working. I can't... remember... anything."

"Anything?" Grawf rumbled, sounding somewhere between surprised and skeptical.

"*Everything,*" Mazel escalated, ears still clamped tightly against her head. "Everything that I didn't live through inside this body—it's all gone... all the memories..." She tried to pull her paws away from Unari; she wanted to claw at her skull where the Rheun chip lived. She wanted to turn the chip back on or, at least, poke at it like one might pick at a scab until it tears away, leaving the wound worse than before. More likely to fester and get infected.

But Unari did not let go. "Didn't it take brain surgery to implant your Rheun chip?"

Mazel nodded, still pulling with slight, jerking sensations at her paws.

Unari continued: "And isn't it an ancient piece of arcane computer technology?"

Mazel nodded again, letting her arms go limp. Her ears tilted a little up from her head.

"Then I don't think you can turn it on by clawing up your skin," Unari said. "It's safe inside your skull, right? So, we'll have Doctor Jardine... or my husband—I don't know whether you'd have an engineer or a doctor fix it—but either way, we'll have them look at it when we get home. To our own galaxy. But first--" Unari stared into Mazel's eyes; her green eyes burned with intensity. "--we have to get back there."

"And out of here," Grawf added. "And you're our commanding officer. So get to commanding."

Mazel was startled by Grawf's blunt tone, and she could

hear the undertone: *"Or else, I'll relieve you of command."* But she wasn't used to being a commanding officer. She'd been an ensign when the Rheun chip had been implanted in her brain, and all of the experience she'd had as a lieutenant felt half-lived. She hadn't done any of it—not Mazel Tabbith.

"I..." Mazel wanted to hand the mission over to Grawf, but the bear was staring at her in a way that challenged her pride. And cats tend to be proud. Even the ones who feel small and lost.

Mazel stood tall, swished her tail, and forced her ears to turn forward. "Right, then, what are our options?" she said, stepping away from Unari and reclaiming her paws for herself. She clasped her paws together behind her back, digging her claws into her own paw pads to keep herself from reaching up to the base of her skull again. She wanted to, oh, she wanted to. But she needed to leave the silent chip alone, safely cradled inside her cranium. She needed to get out of here and put herself in the paws of that pretty squirrel doctor and the white dog wizard. She needed to know what she was up against: "Also, tell me about these—what were they called? Carapids?—again."

"Insectoid warriors," Grawf rumbled, crossing her arms. "Their bodies are basically exoskeletal shells of armor. Their pincer-like appendages and mandibles are built-in weapons." The bear's round ears couldn't flatten like a cat's or some dogs', but Mazel was sure they would have flattened if they could have.

Grawf continued: "They boarded *Star-Skipper 1* as soon as we reached the chosen star system. We hadn't even had time to send out a welcoming message to introduce ourselves." The bear's countenance was remarkably calm given their circumstances, and Mazel thought that ursines, in general, might have particularly good poker faces. The thought felt like it should connect to a memory... but disconcertingly... it didn't.

"Did they say anything?" Mazel asked.

"No," Grawf said. "They fought. They attacked. They bludgeoned. I was the last of us to lose consciousness. Also the first to regain it." Grawf looked away from the others; the big brown bear stared into the mid distance, somewhere between the floor and the farthest wall, which wasn't very far. For all of her bulk and strength, she looked as helpless and lost as Mazel felt. "When I awoke, we were here. The other two—the uncooperative insect and the domineering bird— were gone. I don't know what happened to them."

Mazel noticed that the bear's chain mail sash was missing, and that caused her to reach into her own pocket. Doggarnit, her antique scanner was gone, too. *Why had she owned such an antique scanner anyway? She couldn't remember that either...* She touched a paw to her chest, and yes, the comm-pin had been removed from her uniform. Except it hadn't been removed nicely; it had been torn off, leaving a ragged hole where an orange patch of her fur poked through.

She saw that the comm-pins been removed from Grawf and Unari's uniforms as well, also leaving behind tears. Mazel couldn't see Quincy's breast with the way he was sprawled on the floor, but then he'd never had a comm-pin in the first place, since he wasn't a Tri-Galactic Navy officer.

"Anything that might have been a useful tool for escaping or fighting warrior insects has been taken from us," Mazel hissed in frustration. Except... Mazel looked at Quincy again. The frog was still ash gray like the concrete floor. "Wait, how does Quincy's suit work? Is the fabric of his suit something we could use?"

"You mean, like as a... disguise?" the bear rumbled with obvious distaste.

Did the ursine people of Ursa Minuet dislike subterfuge? Mazel wondered. The calico cat felt sure that she should have known... But she didn't. She missed her long, complicated wealth of memories. Being joined with the Rheun chip had been like inheriting super powers. She hadn't appreciated it enough at the time.

The black cat approached the snoring frog and snagged one of the tattered edges of his suit with her claws. Where she touched the ash gray suit, the fabric bruised black to match the color of her paw. "No, I see what you're saying—this is smart fabric, probably using nanobots to change color. If my husband were here, he could reprogram them to... I don't know." She dropped the tattered edge of fabric and sat down on the concrete ground with her long tail wrapped around her. "He'd make something amazing out of nanobots, a crust of bread whenever they get around to feeding us, and sheer genius."

"I'm sure he would," Mazel said, trying to sound comforting. But she had no idea what it felt like for Unari to be separated from her canine husband by multiple galaxies. Mazel had never been married. Hell, she'd never even been all that deeply in love. In fact, none of her relationships—each with gray-striped tomcats—had lasted very long. Usually no more than a few months. "But look, even without O'Neill's wizardry, we're going to find a way out of here and get back home."

Unari smiled weakly; a smile that lifted her whiskers, but didn't reach all the way to her sad green eyes.

Mazel shoved the snoring amphibian gently with a hind paw, until he rolled onto his side. His eyes snapped open, and his throat bulged with a fit of hiccoughs. Before he'd fully recovered, Mazel asked the frog: "Quincy, do you know how to program your suit?"

"My-- my suit?" The frog pulled his large hind legs under himself, moving into a crouching position, and then felt all over his body with his webbed hands. "Oh, no, my beautiful suit! My poor, poor, beautiful suit's in terrible condition!" He fiddled forlornly with the ragged edges, caressing them ever so gently with the bulbous tips of his webbed fingers.

"Yes," Mazel agreed, "but it still works. And it's the closest thing to a tool or weapon that we have."

Quincy swelled out his neck like a balloon, and let the air out slowly. When he'd returned to his normal size, he said, "I had the tailor, a Reptassan fellow, program my suit for me. I only needed it to match my skin—nothing fancy, no fractal patterns or videos."

Grawf groaned, and it sounded like a very judgmental building settling into its foundation. Unari simply rolled her sparkling green eyes and muttered something about missing O'Neill.

"Are you saying you don't know how to reprogram it?" Mazel asked, trying to stay focused on the task at hand and not get distracted too much by the Phiboon's stunning uselessness. Perhaps if the Carapids returned, he could distract them by playing Chanster's Claws with them... except that all of the game pieces were presumably still aboard their shuttle.

"Well..." Quincy equivocated. "The tailor insisted that I watch while he programmed it. He said only a fool would wear smart clothes without knowing how to properly program them. I didn't appreciate that much... But I could see I wasn't getting out of his tailoring shop until I let him give me the introductory lecture."

"So you *do* know how to reprogram your suit?" Mazel pressed.

"I guess..." Quincy muttered, pulling at his collar, twisting it around so he could look at the tag in the back. "I can see how much I remember. Why? What do you want me to program it to do?"

Mazel hadn't thought of that yet—the obvious choices were all distractions. Fire, so the Carapids would have to scramble to put the fire out; a hole in the ground, so the Carapids would think they'd already escaped; a mirror, so the Carapids would fight themselves. No, those ideas were all dumb. "Just show me what you remember," Mazel said, "and we'll figure something out."

So Quincy pulled his shirt over his head, and he showed Mazel how the tag in the back of the collar controlled the suit's color patterns. While they were working on programming the shirt to display episodes of the Earth sitcom *Small Dog, Big Heart,* the heavy concrete door swung open with a grinding sound. Concrete scraping against concrete. The sound hurt Mazel's head, deep in her jaw. But she kept her senses together well enough to stuff Quincy's shirt—colorfully displaying a heart-wrenching scene where the eponymous small dog was reunited with a long lost brother—inside her own jumpsuit to hide it. She didn't want any Carapid guards seeing there was more to the fabric of Quincy's suit than they'd realized.

Once the heavy concrete door was fully open, Neera hopped through, feathers looking dull, and her bright purple uniform torn in several places. Behind her stood two Carapid guards—their hulking forms dwarfed Neera, and their bodies seemed to be made entirely from plate mail armor, pieced together perfectly to bend with an elastic fluidity, and a frightening array of axes, scissors, and shears that were apparently limbs. Their eyes were faceted gemstones that reminded Mazel of the multi-faceted eyes seemingly always hidden under Omoleura's false chin.

Omoleura had hoped to find zir own origins in this galaxy. Could these brutish, bulky warriors be related to Omoleura? The security chief was so much slighter than them, and yet, zir body changed drastically at times. These insects could be related to zim.

One of the Carapids shoved Neera forward with a brutal blow to her back with a closed pincer. The bird lost her footing and fell to the floor, but she'd been shoved far enough forward that the Carapids were able to close the giant concrete door behind her.

Neera barely waited for the door to finish shutting before she said, "What's the plan? I mean, I assume you're already working on getting out of here..."

Mazel pulled Quincy's shirt back out from inside the belly of her jumpsuit. The crumpled fabric showed a distorted scene of two small dogs and a tabby cat in a coffee shop. Mazel recognized the scene; it had been groundbreaking at the time.

Lieutenant Unari approached her and put a paw on the suit's fabric, smoothing it out. "I remember this..." Unari said. "This is the scene where Vanessa finds out her long lost brother is married to a cat... I loved that episode. It meant so much to me."

Mazel supposed a lot of kittens had grown up watching *Small Dog, Big Heart*. She certainly had. "Yeah, me too," she agreed. Although, she imagined the scene had meant even more to Unari. Even so, the show had legitimatized inter-species marriages at a time when they were still very much taboo, and even more so, it had introduced a cat who became a lead character on a prime time television show. It had been a big deal to a lot of cats.

"I guess I was wrong," Neera twittered sourly. "You're not making escape plans. You're entertaining yourselves while accepting your unfair incarceration. In other words, aiding and abetting your jailors." She grabbed the smart fabric shirt with a feathered hand and yanked it toward herself. "Give me that."

"Hey," Mazel said. "That's the closest thing to a tool or weapon that we have."

"No kidding," Neera agreed, already busily messing with the tiny fabric control panel on the tag. "I must have repro-grammed hundreds of these during the war."

"Really?" Mazel asked.

"Oh, sure," Neera agreed. "They make great bombs. Smart bombs even." The fabric melted in her feathered hands, losing all structural coherence, and dripping between her pinions like mush. Then it squelched back together, forming the lumpy shape of a ball of unbaked bread dough. It even had a similar pale color. "Now we just need a sample of Carapid DNA," Neera said. "Once I prime this thing to attack our enemies, we can each take a glob. When the Carapids come near, pull off a tiny amount—no bigger than a waltan berry—and throw it at them. Bam. No more Carapids."

"That sounds brutal," Mazel observed.

Neera tilted her feathered head. "Does it? Does it offend the little Tri-Galactic Union kitty's finer sensibilities?" Her tone dripped with mockery. "Well, then I guess you can just sit on your tail in this cell forever and rot. But me, I'm getting out of here, and I'm getting that shuttle craft back, and I'm flying with the grace of the Unhatched home."

"Sounds good to me," Grawf rumbled.

"So when the Carapids come back--" Neera began explaining a plan for getting a sample of their DNA, but the bear cut her off by spitting a black twig out of her mouth and handing it to the bird with a large brown paw.

"What-- what's that?" Neera asked.

"A piece of a Carapid's antenna," Grawf answered. "I bit it off. Thought I'd keep it as a trophy."

"And you were keeping it in your mouth???" Quincy galumphed in horror. "Ewww!"

Grawf shrugged. "It tasted kind of coppery. Not bad."

Neera shoved the shiny black piece of Carapid antenna into the putty-like glob of smart fabric. "Perfect," she said. "Now, as soon as the Carapids come back, we can get out of here."

"Great," Mazel said. "Do you know where they're holding Omoleura? We need to rescue zim."

"No we don't." Neera's voice took on a chilly quality.

"We're not leaving a member of our team behind!" Mazel objected.

"Omoleura has betrayed us." Neera turned away from the others. "I saw it with my own eyes. Zhe met zir people, and zhe had no more use for the rest of us."

"Wait," Grawf rumbled, "are you saying that weird chameleon of an insect is related to these impressive warriors?"

"They're probably members of different castes in the same species," Unari said. "You know, like worker, soldier, and queen ants."

"Are you saying Omoleura is a queen?" Grawf asked. The bear sounded incredulous.

"Or some other caste," Unari said. "With a sentient, space-faring species, there could be far more complicated castes than with sub-sentient Earth ants."

"Are you sure Omoleura wasn't playing along with the Carapids?" Mazel asked. "Buying time to help us escape?"

Neera shook her head. "I saw zir order our deaths and begin planning an invasion of our galaxy. We have to warn the Ap-- I mean, Captain Bataille. May the Unhatched protect us all."

"That bilge-toed bastard!" Quincy swore.

Mazel felt a sinking sensation in her stomach. If the Ennea galaxy became a threat, then the nexus to it might be sealed, ending the possibility of any further visits. And for some reason, that made her deeply sad. She had come here for a reason... some bigger, more personal reason than mere science. But... She couldn't remember what it was.

Regardless, Mazel had to defend all of the societies of the Tri-Galactic Union. If these Carapids posed a profound threat, then Neera was right. Captain Bataille must be warned, at all costs.

CHAPTER 8
A DIFFERENT PERSPECTIVE

Rheun's reality shrank down to a pinpoint—pure thought, no physicality. Time could only be measured by the shape of her impatience, which came in waves. With no external anchors, only darkness, it was hard to keep track of who she was. Mazel the cat? Darius the dog? Augrula the bear? An octopus? Maybe even human.

When reality returned, the truth of being Mazel melted away like frost in sunlight. The cat was only a memory, and the physical truth of Rheun's existence had changed. Zhe extended an arm to look at zir paws, but instead two limbs moved—a wing and an arm, zhe thought—and the appendage that appeared in zir view was not a paw. A talon, perhaps; covered in blue fuzz with darker ridges, creating a feathery pattern. Except the talon appeared dozens of times in overlapping, multitudinous views until Rheun figured out how to resolve all of the images into one.

Then zhe began giggling uncontrollably, and zir own voice sounded like a cello tuning. And zhe thought that was the strangest way to think of zir own voice... Omoleura had never thought about the sound of zir voice before. And zhe was quite sure zhe'd never heard of a cello, and yet now, the word conjured images of elegantly curved wooden instruments with long strings.

Huh. Omoleura didn't mind that comparison. In fact, it was quite flattering and made zir feel like singing. But zhe was still giggling and couldn't seem to stop the bubbling fit of laughter from vibrating through all of zir legs and wings.

As Omoleura laughed, zhe felt an itch all over zir body, especially in the crevices between zir exoskeletal joints. An itch that usually meant it was time to spit up the gummy silk from zir mouth for building a chrysalis. Time to meta-morphose.

Rheun wiggled zir arms and legs and wings, trying to shake off the feeling. Zhe was Omoleura Rheun now, and zhe didn't need to metamorphose to look more like a calico cat. That part of zir life was over. For now.

Although, Rheun felt a strange eagerness to undergo an experience first-hand that Omoleura had already lived through so many times that zhe tried to put it off as long as possible each time, like a calico kitten trying to stay up past her bedtime to watch a sitcom about the love affairs of a Maltese dog.

Egg shells! Omoleura's mind was a mess of confusing metaphors and memories right now. Zhe felt excited by the experience of stretching out zir own limbs, just to feel them bend in new places, as if zhe hadn't been living inside this body zir whole life!

And zhe couldn't stop thinking about a birthday party for a puppy who had apparently been zir own son—strawberry cake with peanut butter frosting; brightly lit candles; and a bicycle that zhe'd wrapped zirself in paper that kept tearing until zhe'd used up a whole roll of it. The puppy's smile when he'd opened the bicycle had been enough to melt anyone's heart.

Except Omoleura had never been to a party like that in zir life. Zhe'd been raised by the Avioran scientist who found zim, and Aviorans didn't celebrate their Hatch Days that way. Yet now zir memory was full of those birthday parties—years' worth of birthday parties for a puppy zhe'd never met. And even for zirself, as a kitten. And a puppy, but longer ago.

Unhatched's blessings! Omoleura couldn't believe how calm and restrained Mazel had been, if this was what it had been like inside the calico cat's brain.

Omoleura hadn't understood what zhe was signing up for when zhe had asked the Mimminoi to insert the Rheun chip in zir own brain. And yet, a sense of gratefulness... calmness... self satisfaction? A warm feeling settled over Omoleura's body as zhe remembered the great danger that zhe'd been in —that the Rheun chip had been in. If the Mimminoi had sent the Rheun chip away to the nearest Triloi's laboratories to be studied, then Mazel and Rheun would never be reunited.

At least this way, there was a chance that Omoleura could keep Rheun safe, inside of zir own brain, until the chip could be returned to the calico cat.

And Omoleura could become zirself again. *No offense,* zhe thought. Except... no offense to whom? To zirself? *Zhe was so confused...*

Omoleura remembered thinking of all of these voices and memories in zir head—which had only been in zir head for a few moments now—as imaginary friends. Advisors. Companions. Back when zhe had been Mazel. That little cat certainly had a whimsical way of thinking of the world—so optimistic and creative. And suddenly, a mystery that zhe had been living with for a year—or that zhe had only encountered seconds ago?—was solved.

Now that Rheun could remember his life as Darius and all of the times he'd interacted with the funny little calico ensign —without those memories being directly colored by Mazel's experience of them—zhe remembered how impressed zhe'd been by Mazel Tabbith. She'd been the only choice he'd have ever considered for inheriting himself... his Rheun chip. *Plum-*

meting wingless eggshells! Omoleura needed to rescue that little cat, and get this ancient biohazard of a computer chip out of zir brain.

"Is the Eminent Chrysaloi experiencing negative side effects from zir... *interesting* choice to undergo brain surgery?" asked a high, piping voice. Like a violin.

Omoleura recognized the voice—the Mimminoi who had been assigned to shadow zir, theoretically acting as zir personal assistant. But also possibly keeping the stray Chrysaloi in check.

That was Omoleura—a stray Chrysaloi. Because while half of Omoleura Rheun's quest to discover zir origins had failed so far—there was no sign of a civilization of neural-chip enhanced octopuses—the other half had been a spectacular success. Of a sort. Omoleura was a Chrysaloi of the Hiviiarchy who had hatched from an envoy egg.

The Hiviiarchy explored new and already inhabited star systems by sending out envoy eggs. When the incubating Chrysaloi hatched, they found themselves perfectly designed to blend into any society they discovered. Through metamorphosis and mimicry, they could infiltrate the societies of any sentient life forms they encountered. And then when the Hiviiarchy descended, they had Chrysaloi on the inside, ready to share their gathered intelligence.

At this point, Omoleura was the Hiviiarchy's foremost expert on the three galaxies. Zhe could commandeer an army of Carapids, a fleet of Mimminoi, and be on an accelerated path to joining with two other Chrysaloi to become a mated Triloi. Then zhe'd become the supreme ruler of Avia. That's what the Mimminoi assigned to zim had explained.

That was the path laid out for a Chrysaloi who had hatched from an Envoy Egg and so successfully studied an entirely new society. New to the Hiviiarchy. Omoleura could tell from the Mimminoi's readily apparent excitement that this was all meant to be a great honor.

Omoleura had returned home, and zhe'd been crowned a queen.

Except Omoleura didn't want to conquer Avia.

Avia had been conquered enough, and it had hurt for Omoleura to watch the pain and suffering of the Aviorans under Reptassan occupation. The birds deserved freedom. Freedom to rule themselves. Freedom to be themselves.

And Omoleura knew that the Hiviiarchy wouldn't like that answer. So zhe had played along. It had broken zir three hearts to watch Neera Jerysha's face as the bird became truly convinced that their friendship had meant nothing to zim, that zhe could order her death without a second thought.

From what the Mimminoi had explained to Omoleura, death row was the safest place for zir friends on this lunar installation. No one would dare injure prisoners being held for execution by the Triloi. No matter how dimwitted and dangerously aggressive the warrior Carapids seemed, they would never cross their beloved queen mother Triloi.

Omoleura could experience that same kind of blind love and devotion directed at zirself, if zhe would only accept two other Chrysaloi as zir mates...

But zir three hearts belonged entirely to Neera Jerysha.

The Mimminoi's voice sang out again. "I will summon the brain surgeons again—we will remove the Roooon chip. It is clearly damaging the Eminent Chrysaloi!"

"No," Omoleura said, gathering zirself together well enough to rise from the silky, woven hammock where zhe had been laid out for the surgery. "The Rheun chip is working fine, and my memory has been greatly enhanced, exactly as expected." Well, perhaps not exactly, but Omoleura hardly needed to share the details with a Mimminoi.

Feeling the swaying of the hammock rustling zir wings, Omoleura impulsively fluttered the membranous appendages and almost broke into fits of giggles again at the sensation. Zhe had never had wings before! Except... of course... for every other day of zir life, since zhe had emerged from zir very first chrysalis.

Now *there* was an experience that should be celebrated with peanut butter cake and paper wrapped bicycles! Emerging from a chrysalis for the first time had been Omoleura's physical state of achieving adulthood. But instead of sugary desserts and recreational wheeled contraptions, the day had been marked with brain scans, agility tests, and general scientific poking and prodding...

No matter. Omoleura could hardly blame the Aviorans for their curiosity. Zhe felt a fair amount of curiosity about zirself as well. Or was that Rheun?

Regardless, Omoleura's first chrysalis emergence had eventually been celebrated anyway—not with an Earth-style birthday party, but still. When Neera had learned of how Omoleura had been treated by the scientists who raised zir, she had surprised the chief with a proper Hatch Day commemoration featuring brightly colored flower crowns and necklaces of edible seeds strung in long, looping strands. They'd spent hours together stringing the seeds in patterns, nibbling them away, and stringing them again, all while sharing stories—mostly told by Jerysha. It had been a lovely and unexpected day. Zhe could have listened to that spunky bird tell stories forever.

Neera Jerysha had always been more than kind to Omoleura. Zhe loved the bird dearly.

To keep her safe, right now, Omoleura needed to focus on the present moment, rather than picking over the many strands of zir memories like the seeds on a Hatch Day string. Omoleura had power here, and zhe needed to learn its limits and its uses.

"Come," Omoleura said, "now that I'm ready, I'd like to be shown around the installation. I have much to learn before meeting my mates!"

Omoleura had never been comfortable with deception; zir

intense interest in honesty had been part of what drove zir into law enforcement. And so zhe was surprised how easily the deceptive words shivered out of zir vibrating limbs now. Perhaps, somewhere along the way over zir long history of lifetimes, Rheun had developed a facility for untruths. Omoleura wasn't entirely comfortable with being more comfortable with lying... but zhe had to admit, it would come in useful as long as zhe was behind enemy lines in the galaxy Ennea.

The Mimminoi vibrated its translucent oval wings in excitement, and its long antennae bent forward, almost reaching toward Omoleura. The greenish insect looked much like a praying mantis—another image that was new to Omoleura via the wealth of memories in Rheun.

Like a praying mantis, the Mimminoi's narrow green thorax swelled into a gracefully long yellow abdomen; its large multifaceted eyes and small mandibles gave it a demure, triangular face; and all of its limbs bent steeply, meaning it could have stood quite tall with them all stretched out.

"Indeed!" the Mimminoi exclaimed. "There is much for your Eminence to learn! It's very exciting!"

This particular Mimminoi had clearly decided to attach its fate to Omoleura's. If it could convince the new Chrysaloi from the triple galaxies that it was an essential advisor, then perhaps it could secure a more powerful position for itself when the Hiviiarchy moved on Avia.

The Mimminoi's self-interested motives were painfully clear. Omoleura would have to make the best of them.

"What did you say your designation was again?" Omoleura asked the Mimminoi.

"Batch 59, 4th Hatched." The Mimminoi's antennae waggled proudly. "That means I'm called 59-4."

"You're doing a wonderful job of re-integrating me into

my... true home, 59-4," Omoleura said. "Do... I have a... different name? A truer one?"

"No, no, no, my dearest Eminence!" the Mimminoi exclaimed. "Envoy Chrysaloi are meant to adapt to the societies where they hatch, and so each one returns to the Hiviiarchy with a name in the style of the culture that they've infiltrated and intend to conquer." After a moment's consideration, 59-4 added, "Of course, not every Chrysaloi's deployment is as wildly successful as yours. Your mates—who I'm told are already on their way!—of course, will not be keeping their own names when they join with you, since you will all be returning to this resplendent new galaxy together!"

"Wait, what do you mean—join with me?" Omoleura asked, hesitant. Zhe knew that zhe was merely playing along with the Mimminoi for information, and yet the mere idea of joining zir mind with even more minds was nearly more than zhe could handle.

"Oh, it is quite joyous!" 59-4 exclaimed, clasping its two largest talons together. It truly did look like it was engaged in heavenly prayer. "The three of you will build a chrysalis together—your last one! And when you emerge... oh! Oh! You will be a Triloi!"

"But... practically speaking... What really is a Triloi?" Omoleura couldn't imagine sharing zir chrysalis with anyone else. Ever. It was the most private place and experience that zhe'd ever known. In all of zir lifetimes, and right now, zhe had experienced a lot of lifetimes...

59-4 practically vibrated in ecstasy as it described the different Triloi it had seen holo-projections of—the common thread seemed to involve a multi-part body with a long egg-laying abdomen in the back; at least a dozen different limbs; and a fore-body that maintained some of the mimicked aspects of the species who had influenced the three joined Chrysaloi before they'd become one.

The way that the Mimminoi spoke of Triloi reminded

Omoleura of sermons zhe'd seen Avioran Vees give on the divine nature of the Unhatched. Except apparently, this insect's gods were real. And Omoleura could become one of them.

Omoleura was stopped short by suddenly realizing two things at once: One, zhe had truly believed in the Aviorans' Unhatched until only minutes ago; when zhe had prayed to them, those prayers had been more than mere words, mimicking the words of those around zim. And two, zhe no longer believed in them. At all.

Omoleura thought wryly, *what a strange gift to receive from joining one's mind with an extremely long-lived, ancient computer chip: too much life experience to believe in gods anymore.*

Omoleura wondered if zir belief in the Unhatched would return when the Rheun chip was removed. Zhe had a nagging, disturbing suspicion that it would not. Can belief in gods ever truly be regained once one has outgrown it? Rheun didn't seem to think so. Omoleura tried very hard to not be sure. But it's hard to retain childlike naivete and wonder in the face of years of experience.

And suddenly Omoleura felt like giggling again: zhe never thought of zirself as childlike before. Even when zhe had been a freshly hatched grub, before zhe'd even metamorphosed.

"I have so much to learn..." Omoleura mused, pacing the length of the small medical room.

"Actually, my Eminence," 59-4 said, "you are far advanced from where we would expect an Envoy Chrysaloi to be on zir first day returned to the Hiviiarchy."

"Is that so?" Omoleura asked, genuinely surprised. Zhe stopped pacing in front of a mirrored work table and looked at zirself in the reflective surface. 59-4 came to stand beside zir.

Omoleura could see the resemblance between them—the fine hairs on their carapaces; the fundamental anatomical structure. And yet their coloring and the shape of their different parts were so disparate that it was still hard to believe zhe was one of these strange insects.

Omoleura thought of zirself as a bird.

"Indeed!" 59-4 exclaimed. The praying mantis seemed to be constantly excited. Omoleura supposed it must be very exciting for it to have been the first Mimminoi to discover—and thus ally itself to—a Chrysaloi Envoy from an entirely new galaxy.

Regardless, the Mimminoi's excitement made Omoleura feel even more tired, and today had already been a very long day—filled with centuries of new memories to sort through and an entirely new galaxy.

"Most Chrysaloi Envoys only speak the language of their infiltrated societies when they return home," 59-4 said. "I was actually quite surprised when you spoke in perfect Hiivon to me. The surgeons tell me that there are tiny robots in your brain that must be responsible."

"Ah, yes," Omoleura mused. "Translator nano-bots." All Avioran officers had had the nano-bots injected into themselves after the planetwide vote was decided positively to join the Tri-Galactic Union. Well, a few officers had refused. They had been asked to resign.

Omoleura found the nano-bots incredibly useful, and zhe wished that zhe'd had them during the years of the Reptassan occupation. Many of zir unsolved cases might have actually been resolved if zhe'd had a greater ability to understand the Reptassans. As it was, Omoleura was good with languages, but the Repatassans had still been able to confuse zir and speak around zir knowledge when they wanted to hide information.

Omoleura didn't believe in hiding information.

Well... not usually. Right now, zhe vaguely wished that Rheun's memories could be hidden away. Ideally, back inside that calico cat's head.

"The Triloi of our sector will be most grateful when you share the technology!" 59-4 said.

The Mimminoi's statement sent shivers through all of the fine filamented hairs over Omoleura's carapace.

If zhe was not careful, Omoleura could become a spy and traitor to zir entire galaxy. Zhe did not want the Hiviiarchy to become zir new home. But if zhe betrayed the Tri-Galactic Union and Avia—well, mostly Neera—then there would be no other home for zir to return to.

"These translation nano-bots will be a most useful advancement, Eminent Omoleura, and your ascendance as Triloi over the newly discovered sector will be doubly—no triply!—assured," 59-4 continued in a staccato, allegro voice like a violin dancing its way through a symphony solo. "Why, between revealing the location of the nexus passageway, providing this incredibly useful technological advancement, and your intimate knowledge of the most relevant peoples in the new galaxy, you will most likely become the youngest Chrysaloi ever to ascend to Triloi of a new sector!"

Omoleura was profoundly grateful that zhe'd seen Grawf crypto-locking the shuttlecraft computer's memory during the fight with the Carapids. If the bear had not been so savvy—and physically strong enough to withstand the Carapids' attacks for so long—then the location of Nexus Nine would not be a secret that Omoleura could keep from the Hiviiarchy.

Omoleura had underestimated the bear. When they all returned to Nexus Nine Base, perhaps zhe would consent to rearranging the security shift schedules to incorporate more Tri-Galactic Navy officers into the station's defense, as Grawf had been pressing zir to do for weeks now.

Omoleura's thoughts strayed to zir future at the station—both as Mazel and as an un-enhanced Omoleura—as zhe followed the eager Mimminoi throughout the small lunar base. It was not an impressive outpost, and Omoleura had trouble caring about learning the precise caste differences between different types of Carapids and Mimminoi, all of whom saluted zir with clacking mandibles and talons as zhe passed.

The short version seemed to be: Carapids were warriors; Mimminoi were administrators. On this lunar base alone, there were whole squadrons of Carapids training in some form of martial arts in dark, dungeon-like rooms, and every squad of Carapids seemed to be supervised by a Mimminoi, watching over their dance-like fighting but not actually participating. Like a conductor in front of an extremely violent orchestra.

The brain surgery to implant the Rheun chip had been done by Mimminoi research biologists. Doctor wasn't the correct term, because as far as Omoleura could tell, the Hivi-iarchy didn't bother with performing medicine on Carapids or Mimminoi. Instead, there were warehouses full of unhatched eggs of every kind, shipped to the lunar base from the nearest Triloi, and they could be hormonally urged into hatching at any time.

A Carapid breaks off one of its talons fighting? Fine, hatch a new one.

A Mimminoi suffers a blow to the head and can no longer think clearly due to brain damage? Fine, no problem, hatch a new one.

All the same. All replaceable. So, the surgeons per se were less doctors and more biological researchers, looking for ways to make use of the unique biological assets of any new species they encountered. Again, that was part of why Neera and the others had to be on death row—only a death sentence, setting them aside for murder by Triloi, could protect them from the lunar base's Mimminoi experimenting on them.

Omoleura had been experimented on. Zhe did not wish the position on anyone.

The lunar base's commanding Mimminoi, 59-4, had improvised a cell for Mazel, Grawf, Unari, and Quincy when it had still believed the cats, bear, and frog had somehow kidnapped Omoleura. 59-4 had ordered that Neera be kept separately, as Omoleura's clear mimicry of her form suggested to it that she was the Chrysaloi's attendant. But then Neera had been so defiantly independent, so wantonly disregarding of the supremacy ascribed to Omoleura by the Mimminoi that 59-4 had threatened to have a Carapid snap her neck. That's when Omoleura had ordered her death zirself, protecting her, at least until the local Triloi came.

Omoleura would never want Jerysha's subservience.

But zhe had to admit that 59-4's cloying obeisance was at least convenient. Zhe could see the appeal of commanding a fleet of Mimminois, each of them in command of a squadron of Carapids. Then zhe could truly keep the order.

Except... wasn't that what the Reptassans believed?

Omoleura was reminded of an old Earth saying that zhe'd never known before today: "Power corrupts; absolute power corrupts absolutely."

Besides, Omoleura did not want to spend the rest of zir life laying eggs. Zhe'd already had more than enough children throughout zir long lifetime. No wait, that was Rheun, and those memories would be gone soon, Unhatched willing.

Oh for goodness sake, did Omoleura still believe in the Unhatched, in spite of all of zir first-hand knowledge of how sentient lifeforms have a way of elevating others to godhood —humans, Triloi, imaginary birds that have existed since before the universe began—who do not deserve it? Who are nothing more than other people, fallible, complex, and struggling for meaning, each in their own way?

After the tour of the lunar base and its limited facilities was over, 54-9 brought Omoleura to a small round office with windows all around it, each of them looking out at the night sky. "Until better arrangements can be made, my Eminence," 54-9 said, spreading its serrated, hooked talons wide, "please consider this workspace yours."

"Is this your office?" Omoleura asked.

"Not anymore, my Eminence." 54-9 quickly and surreptitiously removed several objects—possibly personal effects, although Omoleura didn't recognize what any of them actually were—from the work table in the middle of the room. Then the Mimminoi activated a computer display and asked, "Would you like to see images of your intended?"

"You mean... the Chrysaloi I'm meant to join with?" Omoleura asked, feeling an unanticipated and unwanted curiosity. "Yes, yes, I would." Zhe had to answer that way, whether it was what zhe truly felt or not. It was the answer zir Mimminoi attendant would expect. Never mind that it was actually what Omoleura felt...

The Mimminoi tapped at the computer console, and two holographic images appeared, hovering over the workspace, rotating slowly in the air and flickering slightly as motes of dust drifted through them.

One of the images, on the left, looked like a basket of snakes at first glance; a whole tussling bundle of ropy green cords, all tangled together. As Omoleura stared at the image, zhe eventually made out the familiar multi-faceted eyes that all members of the Hiviiarchy seemed to have, buried deep in the bundle of snaky appendages. The snakes themselves seemed to vary—some appeared to be a tattered form of wings with long strands of membranous tissue; others were actual limbs, many-jointed so they bent in many places; and some appeared to be nothing more than decorative spikes of carapace.

"I see you are looking at S'li'thee'tha," 59-4 said, bending its two antennae towards each other until they nearly formed a heart over its head. The Mimminoi couldn't know the cultural significance of that particular symbol to Earth species, but the effect was still upsetting. Patronizing. "Zir infiltrated society was entirely plant-based. Sentient shrubbery! Very unusual! Also, not especially useful to the Hiviiarchy, as it turns out. So, zir chances of becoming a dominant member of a Triloi joining are very low. However! Zir knowledge gained from living among those sentient plants will provide an invaluable... *enrichment*, as it were, to any Chrysaloi fortunate enough to have zir joined to them as a recessive mate. Zhe will make a good partner for you."

Omoleura hummed a noncommittal response, but inside, zhe was deeply intrigued.

The other image, on the right, looked like a sculpture made out of crystal or glass. The Chrysaloi's carapace gleamed like raw diamonds, and zir limbs were elegantly long and narrow. Zir neck swooped like a swan's, and zir wings clustered on zir back like an outcropping of dahlia petals, brightly colored and manifold.

"An extreme beauty, is zhe not?" 59-4 said, noticing that Omoleura's gaze had shifted to the other image. "The Chrysaloi on the right is Karaquen. Zhe infiltrated an insect society. Chrysaloi envoys who infiltrate insect societies are generally quite beautiful—our bodies are built from the same components, and thus other insects are easier for us to mimic."

59-4 eyed Omoleura pointedly, and zhe suddenly felt very self-conscious in zir own faux-avian body. It was true that zir membranous wings were so poorly suited to imitating feathered avian wings that zhe had to combine both wings and folded legs together to imitate the appropriate bulk. But... Omoleura thought zhe had come to imitate the Aviorans quite admirably. Zhe'd certainly spent years practicing. And the Aviorans were a beautiful people with their jewel-toned feathers and gentle curves. Omoleura was proud to mimic them.

Besides, Neera had never made zir feel self-conscious. Neera told zim that zir version of the Avioran form was "adorable." Well, she'd said it once, in zir defense against another Avioran calling zim "creepy-looking," when she hadn't known Omoleura was listening. Even so, Omoleura still treasured the stray word, holding it safe and close to zir three hearts like a lover's keepsake.

Omoleura shifted zir wings and limbs uncomfortably.

"Oh, I'm sorry," 59-4 said. "Have I made you feel self-conscious, my Eminence? Never you worry. S'li'thee'tha and Karaquen will be extremely lucky if you accept their proposals to join with you."

"If I accept them?" Omoleura asked.

"Of course! No matter how beautiful they are, neither of these Chrysaloi has much chance of forming a mated Triloi without you. You have all the power here, my Eminence, for you know more about this new galaxy than anyone else in the Hiviiarchy." 59-4's jointed antennae leaned so close to Omoleura, their bent tips nearly brushed against zir wings, and the Mimminoi's voice lowered to a whispered crooning. "If you do not feel, my Eminence, that these two Chrysaloi will bring you the enrichment that you need to become a fully satisfied laying Triloi in command of a whole sector, then we will search our records exhaustively, find you other options—as many as you need—and reach out to whomever appeals to you most!"

"No, no, they're fine," Omoleura said with a dismissive wave of zir own antennae. Zhe wasn't used to using zir antennae to express emotion, as the Aviorans had no physical analogue to them, and Omoleura had always found that drawing attention to them disconcerted the birds. So, zhe had learned to repress the impulse. However, gesturing with them came naturally to zim now that zhe was speaking with another insect.

"Are you sure, my Eminence?" 59-4 pressed. "The combined features of the Chrysaloi blend together to create the Triloi, and the Triloi's features determine the features of the Carapids and Mimminoi hatched from the eggs zhe lays. If you want to effectively dominate your sector, you must produce healthy eggs that hatch into appropriately designed Mimminoi and Carapids to serve you!"

"I'm sure," Omoleura said in a huskily deep tone, turning away from the holographic display. "Quite sure."

There wasn't a problem with S'li'thee'tha and Karaquen appealing to zim. The Chrysaloi rendered in those flickering holograms were quite beautiful. Extremely appealing. Their images called to Omoleura in a way that even Jerysha's presence did not.

Zhe wondered what it would be like to blend with them—become one creature who had lived as a bird, as a plant, and as an insect. Except... Omoleura had already lived as cats, dogs, bears, humans, octopi... Why did zhe feel such a hunger to know these new forms laid out in front of zir? Was it zir insect self, called biologically to mate with others of zir kind? Or was it zir neural chip self? A seemingly endless well of desire for more and new experiences... Omoleura was not sure, but either way, the desire zhe felt for these two Chrysaloi was immense and troubling.

Omoleura needed to find a way out of here, to rescue zir colleagues and escape... before zhe lost zirself.

CHAPTER 9
CRACKING EGGSHELLS

While Mazel and the rest of her team—minus Omoleura the traitor—waited for the Carapids to return, Quincy lightened the mood by telling stories. Most of the frog's stories seemed to end with the moral: "And so the soggy swamp swallowed them up, along with everything they had and everyone they knew."

After a while, Unari suggested that the rest of them should steal the frog's color-changing pants as well as his shirt and watch captioned episodes of "Small Dog, Big Heart," but Quincy objected both to the idea of being left naked and to the idea of having everyone stare at his legs for entertainment. So, they were left with his swamp stories.

Mazel couldn't help thinking that Quincy's ancestors would have been better off moving out of the swamps, but when she suggested the idea, the frog pointed out that his home world was ninety-seven percent swamp. The remaining three percent was apparently bog.

When the concrete door finally began to scrape open, all five of them tensed—brown bear, blue bird, ash gray frog, black cat, and calico cat. Feline tails lashed; Neera's feathers bristled; Grawf hefted a tiny piece of the smart fabric putty in her paw; and Quincy cowered in the corner with webbed hands over his head. With his camouflaging skin and pants, the curled up frog looked much like a stray boulder.

Mazel saw Grawf eying Quincy, like the bear might like to pick up the cowardly frog and hurl him at whatever Carapids came through the door.

Instead of a pair of obsidian-armored Carapids, Mazel found herself facing Omoleura in zir familiar Avioran form; beside zim crouched an insect that looked like a giant green praying mantis, an insect that looked like a basket of snakes, and an insect that looked like a long-legged swan crossed with an outcropping of crystals.

Would the Carapid-primed bombs even work on these bizarre insects? Were they genetically similar enough? Mazel didn't know, but she did know that it didn't feel right to throw explosives at Omoleura without giving the insect a chance to explain. No matter what Commander Neera believed she'd seen.

Fortunately, during their hours of boredom in the concrete cell, Mazel had planned ahead, arranging several code words for her team. She held her paws out and said, "Grace of the Unhatched's wings..." Then to keep the phrase from feeling stilted and strange to Omoleura, in case zhe truly couldn't be trusted, Mazel added, "...we're so glad to see you again, Omoleura! Can you get us out of here?"

"You can't be serious," Neera squawked, and for a moment, Mazel was sure the bird would disobey her direct order to hold fire. But then Neera folded her wings behind her, keeping her portion of the smart fabric putty carefully tucked out of sight between her feathers, and hopped her way over to one of the empty corners of the cell, twittering tunelessly to herself about betrayals and friendships that could never be repaired.

Omoleura said, "They can't understand us when we speak in our own languages—they don't have translation nano-bots.

"My Eminence," the green praying mantis said, "why are you speaking to the prisoners in this... gibberish? Have your... what did you call them? Translation nano-bots? Have they stopped working."

"No, no, nothing like that," Omoleura crooned sweetly in zir cello-like voice, having returned to the language of these strange, aggressive insects. "I simply had... insults prepared for them, harsh words they'd earned when they thought I was nothing more than a curiosity and not a... fledgling god... which I did not wish to say in front of my betrothed."

"Fledgling god!" the praying mantis exclaimed. "How delightful! How accurate! With your poet's lyricism and the fine qualities that I'm sure your two betrothed will bring to the union --" The praying mantis gestured broadly with its foremost talons at the other two strange insects—the basket of snakes and the long-legged swan. "--why your Triloi will be the greatest, most supernal Triloi of them all!"

Grawf snorted, seemingly unimpressed by this insect's obvious obsequiousness.

Neera squawked, "Betrothed?!?" And then a moment later, she added, "Triloi??? What in the name of everything hatched is that?"

"What is the bird saying, dearest Omoleura?" asked the basket of snakes, coiling and writhing. As Mazel stared more closely at the bizarre insect, she saw that many of the snake-like appendages were antennae, strands of membranous wings, or waving many-jointed limbs.

"She says that she will never forgive me for my betrayal," Omoleura answered.

"Forgive you!" the long-legged swan exclaimed in a voice liking chiming bells. Zhe bent zir graceful neck toward Neera, as if she were trying to get a better look at the bird whom her betrothed had chosen to mimic.

Unlike Omoleura, the long-legged swan's multi-faceted eyes weren't hidden, tucked away where they wouldn't be noticed. They were actually on either side of the small head at the end of the gracefully swooping crystalline neck. "Forgiveness is not hers to give, nor yours to need. The pathetic avian should be grateful—we will make her world orderly. Together."

The tiny, colorful wings on the swan's back fluttered like flower petals in a strong breeze, and she extended two of her long crystalline limbs, one to tentatively touch the basket of snakes and another to Omoleura. The gesture was strangely affectionate.

"Of course, you are right," Omoleura said.

Mazel was beginning to wonder whether she should go ahead and order Neera to throw her explosive putty. Omoleura seemed, at best, conflicted. It might be too late to save the insectile security chief.

"I simply wanted you both to see the creatures who will become our servants in the triple galaxies," Omoleura said to the basket of snakes and long-legged swan. "All of these species are common there."

The basket of snakes said in a voice that hissed like wind over a desert, "You do not need to feel ashamed of the resources that were available to you. Every species has value, even these paltry. We will use their strengths to grow the Hiviiarchy. And exploit their weaknesses."

"You heartless, wingless, piece of powdered eggshell!" Neera swore.

Omoleura responded in a harsh tone, like the squeal of a poorly played cello: "I have the Rheun chip in my brain. Forgive me." Then zir voice changed, sounding sweet and musical again, as zhe switched from the language of Avia to the language of the Hiviiarchy: "I told the bird that she and her entire world would pay for her insults to you."

The basket of snakes writhed, seemingly gleeful at zir betrothed's defense of zir. "Let us go," zhe said. "We can face these puny creatures again, together, once we are joined."

"I feel my chrysalis silk coming in," the long-legged swan said, clacking zir demure mandibles on zir small head. "Gummy and sweet. Ready to build the nuptial--"

Mazel could listen to no more. She cried, "Cracking eggshells!" and hurled a piece of the putty at the praying mantis, since it stood closest to her. Unari hurled a piece of putty at the long-legged swan; Grawf and Neera both threw theirs at the basket of snakes.

None of them threw putty at Omoleura. Mazel didn't know what the security chief's intentions were, taking her Rheun chip for zirself, but she also didn't want to risk damaging it. She wanted her memory back. She wanted her other selves.

The putty exploded, knocking each of the three strange insects backward. Several tendrils blew off of the basket of snakes—in the chaos of the explosion, Mazel couldn't tell if they were limbs, antennae, or merely pieces of membranous wing. The praying mantis's left forelimb tore away, and the long-legged swan lost a leg.

"Don't move," Mazel cried at the insects in their own language, as best she could given the limitations of her feline mouth. "Don't call for your warriors. Don't do a thing."

Mazel had never been in a battle like this before. She'd never seen a person ripped apart by a bomb she'd thrown. Her heart stopped, and she wanted to turn back time, erase the choice she'd made.

But then they'd still be locked in this cell, waiting for the Hiviiarchy to invade their galaxy and subjugate all of the peoples of the Tri-Galactic Union. "Come on," Mazel cried to her team in her own language this time, trying her best to ignore the bizarre swan-like and snaky insects as they writhed, squealing and screeching on the floor. The calico cat led the way out through the concrete door, stepping carefully to avoid the insects' reach. "Let's get out of here, and find our shuttle!"

Glancing back at the far corner of the cell, Mazel added, calling to the shirtless frog, "Quincy! Get up! I'd have Grawf carry you... but I need her to restrain Omoleura."

The bear growled, "*I'd be happy to,*" and grabbed the faux-Avioran roughly by a wing as she headed towards the door. Omoleura was small enough that the bear still had a paw free and said, "Should I drag along this green one too?" She grabbed the praying mantis by the joint above its broken off claw. "It looks like the one that boarded our shuttle with those Carapids. So it *might* know where our shuttle is." The bear's teeth looked mighty fearsome when she bared them. "And if it doesn't--"

"If it doesn't help us," Neera supplied helpfully, "then kapow!" She spread her wings suggestively, fanning out her ruby-tipped pinion feathers. "You lose the other fore talon. Understand?"

"Of course, the Mimminoi doesn't understand," Omoleura crooned irritably from under Grawf's large furry arm. "You weren't speaking its language." But Omoleura was, and so zhe added, speaking to the injured praying mantis, "Guide the death row prisoners to their shuttle craft, 59-4, or else they'll blow off your other talon."

"I don't care!" 59-4 sang like a dying violin. "I will die to protect you, my Eminence! And then you can hatch another of my line, to serve you in our new galaxy!"

"Translate this:" Neera squawked, refusing to even try speaking the Hiviiarchy language with her songbird tongue, even if her nano-bot translators would have let her. "If you don't show us to our shuttle, we will blow up every insect, egg, and scrap of DNA in this shattered eggshell compound. Including your precious *Eminence.*"

Neera was bluffing. Mazel knew Neera was bluffing, because they didn't have enough smart fabric from Quincy's shirt to follow through on her threat. Regardless, the calico cat was frightened by this side of the bird—the way she seemed completely unfazed by the broken insects, writhing in pain on the concrete floor.

Mazel knew Neera had been a freedom fighter, killing Reptassan occupiers as little as a year ago. But watching her face off with these insects made that whole, arcane history more real. She was grateful to have Neera on her side. But she also could hardly believe they were here, standing beside this biological wreckage they had wrought. Yes, they were theoretically facing a horde of insects who wanted to destroy their way of life, but that idea was an abstract future.

The broken bodies, still alive but mangled, those were tangible, physical, reaching toward her with their insectile limbs right now.

Everything Mazel had known in her life, from her kittenhood through her days in the Tri-Galactic Naval Academy and then her handful of years as a full officer, had taught her that problems could be talked out, solved through diplomacy.

Neera hadn't lived that kind of life. Neera was better prepared to face this sort of conflict. Mazel felt a numb calmness spread over her feline body, like the tingly warmth of a paw falling asleep when she'd been standing in one place for too long. This didn't feel real. She doubted herself, and her ability to make these kinds of choices: trading lives in the moment for lives in the future. But Neera seemed certain... Mazel would follow the bird's lead.

"Now!" Mazel screamed in the Hiviiarchy language. "Tell us how to get to our shuttle now!" And as she screamed, she threw a piece of putty—the smallest she could tear off—at Omoleura's left hind talon.

The security chief shrieked in pain as the putty exploded against zir claw, leaving a broken stump behind. But the ploy worked: the praying mantis started talking, blubbering really. "No, no, no, don't hurt my Eminence! Go to the left--" It pointed with its unbroken fore talon.

Grawf carried the injured Omoleura under her arm with a

semblance of gentleness, but she dragged the praying mantis who was guiding them, literally letting its long body be pulled across the hard floor by the broken talon gripped tightly in the bear's paw. Blackish blood smeared across the concrete behind it, but it gamely kept directing them as they weaved their way down the corridors.

Eventually, Quincy took pity on the broken, dragging mantis and lifted up the end of its abdomen. The frog hopped after Grawf, keeping the praying mantis swaying in the air, just above the concrete floor.

As they moved through the corridors of the Hiviiarchy installation, Neera kept checking every space they passed.

"Are you making sure the rooms are clear?" Mazel asked, confused by the bird's behavior.

"Looking for weapons," Neera said, bluntly. "I want any Carapids who find us to see that we're armed, without having to throw bits of explosive at them first."

"You won't find any weapons," Omoleura said from zir position under Grawf's arm. "The Hiviiarchy's weapons are Carapids. And they won't fight for you. Only for me. And only if I'm fighting you."

"Are you fighting us?" Mazel asked.

"Shut that traitor's mouth," Neera squawked at Grawf.

The bear shifted her arm to where Omoleura's wings and legs were pinned more firmly in place, so the insect couldn't vibrate well enough to talk any more.

As Neera had expected, the team encountered several pairs of Carapid warriors, patrolling the hallways, before making it to the warehouse where their shuttle was docked. The bits of explosive putty handled each of the Carapids before they could do damage with their bulky talons, but the plucky team of mammals, bird, and frog were running quite low of weaponry by the time their shuttle was in sight.

Quincy feared for his pants, quite loudly. Much more quietly, Mazel feared for their lives.

The shuttle was surrounded by more insects like the praying mantis—their colors and exact shapes varied, but they were all narrower and less imposing than the Carapids. The praying mantis called them—and itself—Mimminoi. And they seemed to be analyzing the shuttle, studying it, trying to understand every aspect of its construction. However, unlike the Carapid warriors who required their talons to be exploded off of them before they'd leave Mazel's team alone, the Mimminoi raised their arms in the air, squealed, and ran away frightened at the mere sight of their fellow insects, broken and crushed under Grawf's furry arms.

Mazel sent Grawf into *Star-Skipper 1* first, in case there were more Mimminoi inside, trying to unlock the cryptography protecting the shuttle's computer. There were. And those ones came running out of the shuttle, screeching in terror too.

Once all of them—calico cat, black cat, brown bear, shirtless frog, blue bird, and two broken insects—were aboard the shuttle, Grawf asked, "What do you want me to do with our prisoners?"

"Omoleura has a piece of me," Mazel said. "Zhe comes with us."

"Zhe could be lying!" Neera squawked. "Leave the traitor here."

Omoleura struggled under Grawf's arm, until the bear eased the pressure against zir enough for the insect to croon, "Jerysha, believe me, I was only trying to protect you! All of you! Please, please, forgive me."

Neera's feathers ruffled, puffing her face into a frightful, spiky sphere.

Mazel ignored her. The angry, spiteful bird wasn't the commanding officer on this mission. Mazel was. "Omoleura," she said, but then she corrected herself, "Omoleura Rheun, what do you want us to do with Mimminoi?"

"If we leave it here," Omoleura said, "it will die. They

don't bother healing Mimminoi or Carapids. Doctors here are only for Chrysaloi—my kind—and Triloi, who are formed when... my kind is mated in threes."

"Then we'll bring it," Mazel said.

Since they were all inside, the calico cat took her seat at the front of the shuttle and began the procedure for launch. Grawf took her pilot's seat beside Mazel, leaving the broken insects to fend for themselves on the shuttle's floor, under Neera's watchful eye and trigger-happy pinion feathers which still held a pinch of the exploding putty. Mazel assumed the bird was too smart to use it inside the shuttle. She hoped that wasn't a foolish assumption.

Once the shuttle was fully sealed and powered up, Mazel gave the order for Grawf to take them home. They had to ram their way out of the warehouse, but the shuttle's force shielding protected it. *Star-Skipper 1* ripped a hole in the side of the Hiviiarchy installation and made tracks towards the distant stars.

After changing course several times, Grawf dropped the shuttle into a minimal power mode for most of the flight back to Nexus Nine, making it far, far harder for them to be tracked. As far as Mazel knew, there were no Hiviiarchy vessels following them, but it was better to be sure and play things as safe as possible.

No matter how careful they were, Mazel had a feeling that everyone on Nexus Nine Base would be jittery, keeping their eyes nervously on the nexus for a long time after they returned with their devastating news of what they'd found in the galaxy Ennea.

"We've arrived at the nexus," Grawf said.

"Take us through, Lieutenant Grawf." Mazel's fur fluffed out around her neck and shoulders in trepidation. She remembered feeling that the passage through the nexus coming here was extremely significant somehow... but she didn't remember how. She resented the knowledge that

Omoleura might remember, if she could overcome her pride enough to ask zim. But that wasn't Omoleura's memory. And Mazel preferred to wait to get it back, vivid and complete inside of her mind, rather than to ask pathetically for it, only to have it filtered through the insect's vibrating wings in a pallid explanation. If the insect deigned to share those scraps of what zhe had taken from her.

"There's something wrong," Grawf said.

"What do you mean?" Mazel kept staring at the viewscreen, waiting for the bright lines of colors to explode. Instead, there was only blackness and the pinpoint diamond spots of distant stars.

"The nexus isn't opening for us." The bear shifted uncomfortably in her pilot's seat, as if she felt responsible for the failure. But Mazel didn't see how it could possibly be her fault.

Mazel looked at the readings on her computer displays. They were in the right spot. The nexus should have been opening for them.

"The Sky Nest..." Neera said in mournfully, tuneful song, "...is gone?"

"Not gone," Mazel said, still checking her readings. "It's here. It just... won't open. So we can't fly through it."

"The Unhatched... have rejected us." Sad birdsong can pierce through the hardest heart. And Neera's voice reflected that the bird was clearly heartbroken.

CHAPTER 10
VISIONS REVEALED

Omoleura heard Neera's sad song, and zhe dragged zirself, limping and in pain, out of the barracks and toward the front of the shuttle. Quincy hopped after zir, galumphing about how the insect was supposed to stay still until the medical foam on zir talon hardened. The frog had replaced his expensive color-changing shirt with a simple synthesized one in plain, bright green.

But Omoleura couldn't stay out of the way when zhe could hear in Neera's voice that something was so clearly wrong.

"What happened?" Omoleura said to the backs of the two cats, the bear, and zir beloved bird.

Neera was apparently too sad to hold her grudge against Omoleura, because she turned to zim and said, "The Unhatched have abandoned us. The Sky Nest won't open."

Omoleura's three hearts opened to her.

"We can't get home if the nexus won't open," Mazel added, glaring at Omoleura. "And I can't get back my memories until we get home." The calico cat's ears flattened. She looked angry, but also adorable.

Omoleura wondered how much Mazel remembered.

Without being Rheun, she might not remember anything about why she'd cared enough about the nexus to have thrown herself across the universe into an entirely different and unexplored galaxy. She probably didn't remember that the Rheun chip was still storing a firewalled vision from their earlier passage through the nexus.

Omoleura wondered if the vision could possibly contain anything helpful for understanding why the nexus wasn't working. Zhe knew that the rest of the team wouldn't let zir download and watch the vision in private right now. None of them trusted zir anymore.

And zhe also knew that Mazel Rheun—and Darius, and many of zir other past selves—had cared deeply about controlling the information that might be in the visions. Zhe still remembered the discomfort of watching the previous vision with Shep and worrying that zir old friend would treat zir differently if he knew about zir past lives as a human. As a god.

But Omoleura Rheun was a god already. Zir subjects had been bowing to zir and planning to commit atrocities on zir behalf only a few hours ago. One of zir acolytes still lay in the barracks, suffering and praying to zir. Omoleura had been listening to 59-4's babbled troths and pleading for favors until the sound made zir vibrate with anger.

If Shep couldn't handle the news of zir past lives better than the mewling sycophant 59-4 handled the fact of zir current life, then perhaps it was not a friendship worth saving.

Of course, it was easy for Omoleura to believe that—no matter how strong zir memories of friendship with Shep were, the truth was that the strongest bond of friendship zhe felt in zir current form was to Neera Jerysha. And zhe was in no danger of discovering—and inadvertently revealing—that zhe was actually a bird deity, older than time itself.

Powdered eggshells. Mazel had shot off zir foot. The

calico cat could deal with the consequences of whatever happened here when she got her memories back. Besides, she might never get them back if Omoleura didn't share what zhe knew.

"I've had a vision," Omoleura said.

All of them turned to look at zir; skeptical, with uncertainty in their eyes.

"Remember in the Temple of Yunib?" Omoleura asked. "How Shep—Captain Bataille—had a vision, and I—uh, Mazel—didn't?"

"Yes," Neera agreed.

"I think I was learning about the bonsai trees at that time." One of Unari's black ears skewed to the side. She looked curious.

Mazel just looked surprised. Her ears had perked up though. She must be curious where this was heading too. "I... remember being there," she said. Then a moment later, after her ears flicked, threatening to flatten again, she added, "Yes, I remember that. I think."

"Except," Omoleura said, "we did have a vision, but the Rheun chip firewalled it."

If Mazel's memories had been more complete, her ears would have flattened here. She would have known that Omoleura was sharing their secrets. But right now, their secrets were secret even from her. She might remember the fact of watching the vision with Shep, but she must not remember the emotional significance.

"We were able to download the memory of the vision," Mazel said. "And watch it. On a video screen."

"That's right," Omoleura agreed.

"Why does this matter?" Mazel asked, clearly unaware of how close Omoleura was treading to revealing things that she wouldn't want revealed... when she was complete again.

Or maybe... maybe she wouldn't care anymore? How much was Rheun being changed by the experience of being

Omoleura? When they went their separate ways, would Omoleura believe in the Unhatched again, and would Rheun feel shattered by having the full history of itself revealed? Or would their effects on each other be permanent?

Usually, the changes to Rheun's personality caused by living as each of zir hosts were permanent. But usually Rheun lived with a host for a lifetime, not a day.

Neera flapped her wings impatiently. "It matters, because every vision from the Unhatched is a gift. If we've rejected their gift by leaving it unopened in some computer chip, then no wonder they won't let us return to the hallowed ground of their sacred temple!"

"So... we should download the memory and watch it?" Grawf asked. "And then, magically, a hyperspatial portal between galaxies will open up for us and let our shuttle fly through?"

Omoleura snapped, "Your people believe in a god made from a swarm of bees and a sentient honey golem. Don't be so superior."

Grawf blinked in surprise. And then the bear broke into deep belly laughter. "You are different with an ancient computer chip in your brain! I like it."

Omoleura felt a weird warmth towards the bear and vaguely, distantly remembered that when zhe'd been a small calico cat, she'd been attracted to the brawny brown bear. At least, a little. Perhaps only subconsciously. Omoleura wasn't sure zhe'd noticed the attraction when zhe'd been Mazel and experiencing it directly, but now she could tell the attraction had been there, because zhe was keenly aware of its sudden absence.

That poor calico kitty, fighting to get back this mess of confusion. Hey, Omoleura thought, that's me that I'm thinking of as a mess of confusion... no it's Rheun, and it will be gone soon... except... not if the "me" that's thinking this is Rheun...

Omoleura shuffled zir wings and shifted zir injured foot talon. The shock of pain in the stump of a blown off foot focused zir. Zhe needed to get back to Nexus Nine Base where that chirpy, over-eager squirrel doctor could heal zir foot properly and do some desperately needed brain surgery.

"Let's look at the vision," Mazel said. "It can't hurt, and I haven't heard any better ideas. Besides, the longer we sit here doing nothing, the more likely the Hiviiarchy is to find us. And if they find us, we have to play chase until we can shake them off of our tails—if we can ever shake them off of our tails. Because we can't go home with them watching."

"Agreed," Omoleura said. "The Hiviiarchy is my own people... and I would not inflict those maniacal insects on the Aviorans or the peoples of the Tri-Galactic Union, even if protecting the birds, mammals, and others of our galaxy meant my own death."

Neera tilted her head. Omoleura hoped she was reconsidering her claims that their friendship could never be repaired. But even if she never forgave zim, zhe would protect her and her world from another subjugation. And based on the squads of Carapids practicing martial arts and the Hiviiarchy's overall callousness towards life—even the lives of their own—possibly a much worse, longer lasting, and wider spread subjugation than the Aviorans had suffered under the scaly claws of the Reptassans.

From what Omoleura had learned during zir hours as a fledgling god, the Hiviiarchy controlled most of this galaxy. Few habitable planets had escaped their reach. And they'd eagerly, hungrily take over any new galaxies made known to them.

With a twinge, Omoleura wondered if the octopuses who had brought zir Rheun-self through the nexus so many eons ago had been fleeing the grasp of the Hiviiarchy. Had the remnants of the society who'd originated half of zirself been destroyed by the society who'd originated zir other half?

Unari arranged for one of the computers to scan Omoleura's brain and download the firewalled memory from the Rheun chip. The memory began playing on the shuttle's main view screen, replacing the empty star field with the strange, pixelated colors of a heat map—lime green, magenta, mustard yellow, indigo, and fiery orange. This time, instead of a shuttle full of zir past selves, the vision showed only one face. A canine face with large triangular ears, and its muzzle moving like it was speaking.

With the colors skewed, it was hard to be sure, but Omoleura thought they were looking at Shep.

"Is that the captain?" Neera asked.

The canine face kept speaking, saying something over and over again. When the sound finally finished processing, the shuttle's speakers played the words, "Bring the Apex. Bring us the Apex. Bring the Apex to us." Over and over.

"Well, *that's* helpful," Unari said wryly, black tail lashing irritably behind her. "The captain's on the other side of the nexus! If these nexus-dwelling god-things wanted us to bring him to the nexus, they'd have to let us back through first."

"Not necessarily," Mazel said, distractedly. The calico cat was already busy checking something on the computer panels around her. "I think, we might be able to send a subspace message through the nexus, even if the passageway won't open wide enough to let our shuttle through."

"You mean, it's open a little bit, even though we can't see it?" Unari asked.

"It's a rip in the fabric of space-time," Mazel said. "There's a limit to how tightly it can close without ceasing to exist altogether."

"Or to have ever existed," Grawf added.

The calico cat looked at the bear in surprise. "You know about the physics of nexus passageways?"

"A little," Grawf rumbled, grudgingly. "I like to study

ahead about every aspect of the assignments I take on. And the nexus is a big aspect of working on Nexus Nine Base."

"I like to do that too," Mazel said. "You can never be too prepared." The calico cat stared at the large brown bear for slightly longer than was strictly necessary before turning back to her computer consoles.

Omoleura felt a complicated mixture of revulsion and sweet anticipation for the romantic possibilities zhe could foresee for herself with Grawf when zhe returned to being Mazel.

"Can you turn that off?" Omoleura gestured with one of zir wing-arm limbs at the looping vision. There didn't seem to be any more to it than Shep asking for zir to bring the Apex, presumably to the Sky Nest. And zhe didn't need to see that particular image any more.

Omoleura wondered if Shep would still call zir "Big Dog" in this form. Zhe hoped zhe'd get a chance to find out. The look on that German Shepherd's face when he realized his old friend Darius was now Omoleura would be priceless. Almost worth the extra brain surgeries. Almost. But not quite.

Grawf turned off the looping image on the viewscreen, and the black sky, lightly dusted with sugar crystals of stars, returned.

"What message are you planning to send through the... nexus?" Neera asked. The bird must be feeling really lost and frightened, and totally dependent on the Tri-Galactic Navy scientists running this mission, if she was calling her people's sacred temple of the gods by its secular name.

"Plain text is the lowest bandwidth style of message we can send," Mazel said. "So I'm sending a simple explanation of our situation—trapped in this galaxy with a non-responsive nexus and an enigmatic message telling us to "Send the Apex"—in an ancient binary Earth language called Morse code."

Neera's feathers ruffled when Mazel called the Sky Nest

"a non-responsive nexus," but she didn't say anything. She kept the objections in her heart. Omoleura had seen the bird react like that to many things that bothered her over the years; usually it meant she was saving her objections up to tell zir about them later, venting and ranting until Omoleura vibrated with amusement. Then they'd both break into laughter.

Omoleura hoped they could have that conversation later. When they were back in their own galaxy, and this chip was out of zir head.

Contrarily, zhe also didn't care at all about having that conversation, and hoped it wouldn't happen until zhe was back in Mazel's head, where zhe belonged.

"There," Mazel said. "The message has been sent."

Omoleura imagined zhe could see a sparkle of color in the blackness of the sky, a faint glimmer of the Sky Nest's usual glory, but it was probably only an illusion caused by staring at the empty sky too hard.

"Did the message go through?" Neera asked, nervously shifting her weight from one talon to the other and repeatedly re-folding her wings behind her back, as if she were ready to fly away at any moment. The bird might have been trapped inside a shuttlecraft, but if willpower alone could have let her wings carry her through the vacuum of space and into the Sky Nest, Omoleura had no doubts she'd have done so. "How long until we know if the Unhatched allowed the message through?"

While waiting for the answer to her question, Neera clacked her beak in a motion that Omoleura recognized as a form of unvoiced prayer. Zhe'd seen whole rooms full of Aviorans clack their beaks in the same way while listening to a Vee preach. Zhe'd also seen Aviorans who'd been thrown in the brig during Reptassan rule clack their beaks in that way for hours, alone in their cells.

Omoleura remembered all too vividly that their prayers

had often gone unanswered. At least, as far as zhe knew. At least... in this physical world.

As Omoleura watched Neera pray silently to her gods, zhe felt a strange sense of responsibility tug at zir three hearts. And zhe limped zir way back down to the barracks.

59-4's antennae waved wildly with excitement as soon as it saw Omoleura. The Mimminoi had fared far worse during the battle in the death row holding cell than Omoleura had. Zhe had lost a foot; 59-4 had lost an entire limb. And before Quincy had foamed over their wounds with medical gel, the Mimminoi had lost a great deal of blood. Omoleura wasn't sure it would survive.

"My Eminence," 59-4 sang in a faint voice. "You have returned."

"Yes," Omoleura said, unenthusiastically but trying to hide zir lack of enthusiasm. "I've returned." Zhe crouched down on the bunk opposite the one where the Mimminoi was spread out, legs dangling off the edge of the cot and wings squashed beneath itself.

But the Mimminoi's multi-faceted eyes glittered, and Omoleura could see zirself reflected in every silvery facet. The expression on 59-4's demure triangular face seemed to take on a more beatific, peaceful expression now that it could see its god. Its whole body relaxed and lay more easily on the cot.

"Have we been rescued yet?" 59-4 asked. The way its antennae kept waving, moving independently of each other, looked uncontrolled. The Mimminoi might not last much longer at all.

And so Omoleura had to consider zir answer carefully. Zhe didn't like lying. But zhe knew that sometimes, there was no reason to share a harsh truth. "I've taken my proper position aboard this shuttle," Omoleura said.

Both antennae pointed at Omoleura for a moment, but

then one strayed away until it lay flat on the cot above 59-4's resting head. "My Eminence, I always had faith in you."

Let the Mimminoi believe what it needed to, Omoleura thought. What zhe said was, "We will be returning to the new galaxy shortly. At least, that's the plan. Would you like to be my deputy there?"

"Deputy?" 59-4 asked. Its other antenna had lain down now too, at an angle to the other one, but its tip also rested on the cot.

"My most important assistant," Omoleura said, telling zirself that the offer wasn't a lie. If the Mimminoi survived, it couldn't be allowed to return to the Hiviiarchy after visiting Nexus Nine Base. But perhaps it could find a place for itself on on the base. With the right training and the right re-socialization...

It was a dream, but it was a nice one. Omoleura liked the idea of the green praying mantis working beside zir. Another insect. Another outcast member of the Hiviiarchy.

"Yes, my Eminence, I would like to be your deputy."

59-4 didn't say anything more, but its breathing grew loud and labored. Omoleura listened to it breathing.

After a while, the Mimminoi said, "Perhaps, it would be best if you hatched a new egg in my line. I think... I am too tired to be your deputy myself. But another in my line..."

"I'm sure your line would serve me well," Omoleura said. Zhe was saved from having to say more by Mazel bursting into the barracks.

The small calico cat had a uni-meter in her paws, and she held it up to the side of Omoleura's head, right beside the eyespots of darkened fuzz. "Hold still," she said.

Omoleura held still, but zhe asked, "Why?"

"If you have another vision, I want to know about it right away," Mazel said, uni-meter blooping and flashing lights in her paw. "So, I'm turning off the firewall inside the Rheun chip. Or trying to." Mazel placed her other paw on Omoleura's folded wing, steadying the insect.

"I miss being you," Omoleura said.

The calico cat stopped, statue still except for the very tip of her tail which twitched.

"This was the only way." Omoleura stared at the cat. Her splotches were backwards—the way they'd look to Darius. By now, Rheun expected to see those splotches reflected in a mirror. They were supposed to be zir own. "Your splotches look backwards to me," zhe said. "I expect to see them in a mirror."

"I miss you too," Mazel said. "At least, I think I do." She lifted her paw from Omoleura's wing and placed it on her own head, like she was fending off a headache. "I feel like I can't see... like I should know so many things... but I can't remember any of them. I feel useless this way." Her paw slipped from her forehead down to the back of her neck, close to where the Rheun chip should be. But wasn't.

"I know you wondered why Darius chose you," Omoleura said, reaching with a talon to take hold of Mazel's paw, and then ease the paw away from the void in her mind. "You are glorious. Brave, creative, full of life, and unstoppable. There is no one else I'd rather be."

The calico cat and the insect stared at each other. Omoleura looked strange to zirself, reflected in the cat's golden eyes.

"Except..." Omoleura said, "...maybe myself without this plummeting chip in my head..."

Mazel laughed.

"By the grace of the Unhatched, I swear," Omoleura said, "I cannot wait to give my Rheun-self back to you, and would never have taken it if there had been any other way."

"I believe you," Mazel said.

"Do you think Neera will forgive me?" Omoleura asked.

"That I don't know," Mazel said. The uni-meter blooped

and blipped a few more times, and then she slipped it back into a pocket. "The firewall should be off now. I... will speak to Neera on your behalf. After everything is over. Okay?"

Omoleura waggled zir antennae in acknowledgment. The gesture felt right, even if the cat probably wouldn't understand it. Zhe didn't feel like trying quite to hard to pretend to be something zhe wasn't anymore. Zhe liked taking on the form of the Aviorans. But zhe was not Avioran. Perhaps, it was time for the people around zim to meet zir halfway.

Mazel left the barracks, leaving Omoleura alone with the fading Mimminoi.

Omoleura still reflected in the Mimminoi's multi-faceted eyes, but the glimmer of life was nearly gone. Zhe waited with zir acolyte in silence.

CHAPTER 11
BIG DECISIONS

The tension aboard the shuttle was palpable. With every minute they waited, Mazel expected a Hiviiarchy warship to find them. When an answering message from Bataille finally came, the Morse code translated to: "Sending probe. Standby."

With bated breath and scanners running, Mazel waited for the probe. Finally, bright lines of color flashed across the shuttle's main viewscreen, dimmer than they'd been before but recognizably an opening to the nexus.

A small, un-crewed probe emerged from the colors, like a silver egg being laid by the universe.

Neera breathed, "*The Sky Nest.* Unhatched lead us home."

"It's too small to fly through," Grawf reported.

But they'd gained a great deal of data by scanning the nexus's reluctant opening. For one thing, the nexus was still open in their own galaxy, even though it was closed here.

That was actually good news.

"The Nexus passageway is only working in one direction," Mazel said.

"But... we got our probe back," Unari said. "When we

tested the nexus before coming here." The black cat's tail was lashing wildly. "What changed?"

"Maybe nothing changed..." Mazel had the shuttle's computer download all of the data that the probe had gathered while flying through the nexus. Then she transmitted instructions to the probe to try to return. "Perhaps, we can't pass through because *Star-Skipper 1* is bigger than the probe."

But the probe failed to pass back through, sitting stubbornly in the black sky like a silver egg that was mocking them, refusing to hatch.

Before Mazel could come up with another idea to try, she heard a wailing cry like a cello being torn to pieces. Omoleura came limping down the shuttle's central corridor, limbs flailing in a way that distorted zir bird-like appearance beyond anything Mazel had seen before. Zir body tilted backward, showing zir multi-faceted eyes more clearly and making the faux-head above them look like a hood that had been pushed back. Zir antennae which were usually hidden, laid flat against zir body, pointed straight toward Mazel.

"Are you having a vision?" Mazel asked, reaching her paws out to take hold of two of Omoleura's talons. She felt even more cut off from her own self now, but then she hadn't been allowed to experience the previous two visions either. But this time, she could see that the insect was in the throes of a powerful experience. "What do you see?"

Neera wrapped a wing protectively, gently around the thrashing insect. Perhaps she would forgive zim after all. "What are the Unhatched showing you?" Or maybe she just wanted to feel close to her gods.

"Send the Apex!" Omoleura screamed, zir entire body vibrating with the words. "Send him! Send the Apex!"

Mazel shook her head and stepped away, letting Grawf take over restraining the maddened insect. "Be gentle," Mazel instructed the bear.

Mazel stared at all of the data in front of her. She didn't see how sending Captain Bataille through the nexus would make a difference. But the cryptic message from Neera's supposed gods was all they had to work with, and Mazel needed to get her team home.

What could the captain have that would make a difference? And what could have changed the nexus since the original probe had passed through it?

As far as Mazel knew, the only significant event to have happened to the nexus since the test probe returned to Nexus Nine Base was when *Star-Skipper 1* flew through the passageway. But there was nothing special about Star-Skipper 1—it was a standard Tri-Galactic Navy, short-term mission, science vessel. The strangest thing about *Star-Skipper 1* was that the Rheun chip was aboard it.

Mazel turned and watched Omoleura flailing, seemingly suffering a seizure as zhe was held steady by Grawf's firm, large paws and Neera's engulfing wings. The bird had wrapped both wings around Omoleura now.

For a moment, Mazel wondered if the nexus would open for them if they left Omoleura—and more importantly, the Rheun chip—behind. Perhaps the presence of the chip was somehow suppressing the nexus passageway from opening.

Would Mazel make that sacrifice? She knew that the Rheun chip was a huge part of herself... but it didn't have to be. She could stay as she was. Leave those memories behind to rot away in the Ennea galaxy. And clearly, Omoleura would be well taken care of here. Zhe had an entire society of worshippers waiting for zir with open arms.

Except if the Rheun chip was what suppressed the nexus, then the nexus would open for a fleet of Hiviiarchy warships, as long as they left Omoleura behind. And Omoleura knew the location of the nexus. Zhe could not be left behind in this galaxy. No matter how much Mazel trusted the insect's intentions now, there was no telling what difference a few years of living among the Hiviiarchy—being celebrated as a god— would do to Omoleura Rheun and zir loyalties.

For goodness sake, Mazel didn't even know how much she could trust Rheun. She couldn't remember who Rheun was... She knew, in an abstract way, that Rheun was a chip who'd lived many lives, passed down from one host to the next... and Rheun had chosen her. But she didn't remember the internal intricacies of those lives. Why, she couldn't even remember the names of any of Rheun's hosts before Darius.

Maybe... leaving Rheun behind was a kind of freedom.

Maybe... it was time for the long-lived chip to die.

But could she sacrifice Omoleura?

"I'm going to ask Captain Bataille to send Doctor Jardine through the nexus on another shuttle," Mazel said, typing the message out in Morse code as she spoke. "I believe the Rheun chip may be interfering with nexus in some way. If the squirrel doctor can remove it from Omoleura's brain, we can discard it, and then we might be able to safely pass back through the nexus passageway."

"Might?" Unari asked uncertainly. "I don't like those odds.

Neera squawked, "The Unhatched aren't asking for some bushy-tailed squirrel doctor. They're asking for the Apex!"

"I don't see how Captain Bataille coming through the nexus will make a difference," Mazel said. The message was already sent.

"When a god asks you for a favor," Quincy said, "you don't pick and choose what parts of the favor you want to do." He crossed his arms over his bright green synthesized shirt. The whole top of his body was bright green to match the synthesized shirt, but his legs blended into the colors of the shuttlecraft around him. He looked like a genie, hovering in the air with nothing below his torso. He hadn't participated much in the previous conversations. He had less of a science background than any of the others and seemed well out of his depth whenever they discussed physics and space-time ruptures.

But he had an opinion when it came to obeying gods that—as far as Mazel knew—he didn't believe in.

Bright lines of color flashed across the shuttlecraft's main viewscreen: sky blue, lemon yellow, auburn, brown, honey gold, every shade of green that appears deep in a forest on Earth, and the silver of a new moon. All of them so bright and brilliant that they looked like the platonic ideal of colors, more real than any color Mazel had ever seen before.

"What changed?" Mazel asked, but none of them knew.

Regardless, another shuttlecraft appeared in the flashing colors, smaller than *Star-Skipper 1*, not a science ship, just a simple two-person transport vessel.

"Fly through!" Quincy cried. His neck swelled up like a balloon.

Grawf dropped her hold on Omoleura, and the insect fell to the shuttle's floor, still thrashing, still embraced by Neera's blue and red wings. But before Grawf could return to her pilot's seat, Mazel had already powered up the engines.

Star-Skipper 1 sailed through the flashing colors, and the other shuttle changed direction, following them back into the mouth of the nexus passageway.

Time and reality dilated around them. And suddenly Mazel was a tiny kitten again. She was no longer on a shuttle. She was no longer in space. Instead of her Tri-Galactic Navy uniform, she was wearing a cozy flannel robe and pajamas with spaceships on them. She was back in her kittenhood home, holding a wrapped present on her lap.

The present was wrapped in silver paper that reflected her face with its lopsided splotches, and on top of the box, ribbons curled in a colorful tangle. She kept pulling the coils of ribbon out, stretching them with her fuzzy paws and then letting them boing back into place. She couldn't decide if she should open the present or not.

A big dog approached her. A German Shepherd wearing a Tri-Galactic Navy uniform. He kneeled down beside the small calico kitten. "You don't have to open it," he said.

"But it's a present," she mewed. "I love presents." Her claws caught in the ribbon and cut off one of the colorful curls with a satisfying zing.

"It will change you," the dog said. He looked familiar, like an old friend she hadn't met yet.

"Everything changes me," the kitten mewed. "Every day I'm taller. My fur keeps getting less fluffy. As I grow, the stretches of white between my patches of orange and black grow, but the orange and black patches seem to stay the same size. So more and more of my fur is white. But I'm still me. Nothing can make me not me."

"Then you should open it. It's very valuable."

The kitten ripped open the silver paper with her claws, tearing a gash down the middle of the reflection of her face. The torn reflection spoke to her, saying, "Always remember: you have a choice."

When she finished tearing the paper away, she opened the box inside and found a toy shuttlecraft. Wait, no, a real shuttlecraft, flying through a ripple in space-time that looked like a river. Time and space flexed outward; inside became outside, flipping along an axis that Mazel had never considered before.

And she found herself on the *Star-Skipper 1* again, fully grown, wearing her Tri-Galactic Navy uniform, and watching the chaos of colorful lines on the main viewscreen. The colors dimmed back into nothing, leaving the blackness of space, broken only by scattered stars and the blue-green gemlike sphere of Avia, orbited by Nexus Nine Base.

An incoming message from the shuttlecraft behind them

replaced the space scene on the viewscreen with an image of Captain Bataille and Lieutenant O'Neill. The two dogs were sitting beside each other inside the small shuttlecraft that had come through the nexus to rescue *Star-Skipper 1*.

"Captain Bataille here," the captain said. "Is everyone aboard *Star-Skipper 1* all right?"

Mazel turned to her crew: Grawf, Unari, and Quincy seemed fine. Neera was on the shuttle floor, kneeling over Omoleura who was twitching, convulsing lightly, and seemed to be halfway covered in chrysalis silk that was still dribbling out of zir mandibles.

"Omoleura seems to be having a seizure," Mazel said. "We need to get zir to Nexus Nine Base immediately for surgery—including surgery to remove the Rheun chip."

"We'll follow you there," Captain Bataille said. "And I'll send word ahead to Doctor Jardine to prep for your arrival."

Mazel nodded. "Thank you, Captain."

Lieutenant O'Neill didn't say anything, but his white bearded muzzle was split in the widest grin, and his short tail was wagging up a storm in his chair behind him. Out of the corner of her eye, Mazel saw the black cat wink at her husband, and his tail seemed to break the laws of physics by wagging even faster in response.

Grawf took over the shuttle's controls and piloted *Star-Skipper 1* back to Nexus Nine Base. When they were fully docked, and the airlock had cycled, a team of Avioran officers came aboard with a stretcher. They strapped the seizing insect, who was now more of a chrysalis than anything else, onto the stretcher and carried zir away.

As soon as the path through the airlock was clear, Lieutenant O'Neill rushed aboard, tail still wagging up a storm. Unari practically jumped out of her fur when she saw him. The black cat rushed into the white dog's arms, and they spun around together, embracing tightly.

Unari and O'Neill left the shuttle, paw in paw, whispering excitedly to each other.

Neera and Quincy gathered the day-trip bags they'd stowed in the small barracks, and on her way out, the bird gently informed Mazel that their prisoner, the green praying mantis, had died. Neera said she would send another team of Aviorans with a stretcher to handle the body.

Mazel and Grawf waited for them to come, and once the praying mantis was gone, it would have made sense to leave the shuttlecraft... go back to living her life on Nexus Nine Base.

But Mazel couldn't seem to muster the willpower and initiative to stand up. She felt overpowered by and lost in the implications of her dream. Why had she seen herself as a kitten, unwrapping a present? Did she not want the Rheun chip back?

Her life would be simpler without it.

"Are you okay, Lieutenant?" Grawf asked. The bear had been sitting quietly, patiently beside the calico cat.

"Just call me Mazel, for now," Mazel said. When she'd inherited the Rheun chip, she'd only been an ensign. She wasn't sure that she should be a Lieutenant without it. Not until she earned the promotion by herself.

"Are you disappointed by what we found in the Ennea galaxy?" Grawf asked. "It seemed like... you were looking for something specific."

"It did seem that way," Mazel agreed. "But I can't remember what I was looking for. So, I don't know if I found it. I think... the Rheun chip was looking for something. But I don't know if I'm Mazel Rheun anymore. I don't know if I want to be."

"You don't have to be," Grawf said.

Mazel stared at the blank view screen of *Star-Skipper 1*. The screen was off and didn't show anything—not even stars. Just the empty darkness of a screen that's offline. A screen where she could almost make out her own reflection in the darkness.

"If I don't take back the Rheun chip from Omoleura, then a creature—a technological creature, but still a creature—will die." Mazel put a paw to her head. She felt dizzy with the weight of responsibility that Darius—no, Rheun—had laid upon her.

"Omoleura won't keep it?" Grawf asked.

"No, zhe told me in no uncertain terms that zhe couldn't wait to have it removed."

"You could give the Rheun chip to someone else," Grawf suggested.

"Who?" Mazel asked. "Who would take it?"

"Probably lots of people," Grawf rumbled. "It's a little bit like being immortal, isn't it? That would make it very valuable."

"A little," Mazel admitted. "But it's also like ceasing to exist at all. And... I can't just give it to anyone who would take it. Anyone who values it for the wrong reasons. I owe Rheun better than that."

"Why?" Grawf asked.

"Rheun picked me."

The bear and the calico cat sat in silence together for a while.

Mazel knew that if she had the Rheun chip in her head, she'd be seeking Captain Bataille out for conversations like this one. She remembered that he was a big part of why she'd come to this station, and she knew how much it had meant to her when he'd called her Big Dog.

But she wasn't Big Dog right now. And she wasn't sure if they'd still be friends if she never became Big Dog again. She'd only known the captain for a week or so as Mazel. If she asked him what he thought, surely he'd want her to preserve the memories and strand of life that remained of his best friend.

Except... he had been in her dream, and he'd told her that she had a choice.

"Would you like to get some dinner?" Mazel asked. "Or breakfast? I'm not really sure what time of day it is... I'm not really sure of a lot of things right now."

"Dinner sounds good," the bear rumbled.

And so Mazel spent the evening with someone who had never met her as Mazel Tabbith and had barely known her as Mazel Rheun. Someone she could just be Mazel with. Lost, confused, memory-full-of-holes Mazel.

Grawf cooked a meal for Mazel in her quarters, and while the bear prepared the food, the calico cat looked at the bear's belongings and asked her about them. Grawf had a whole set of curved swords hanging on her wall. They looked a lot like a curved sword that Mazel remembered hanging in her own quarters when she'd arrived on Nexus Nine Base.

Why did Mazel own an Ursine-style sword? Rheun would know.

Grawf told Mazel the history behind why the swords were curved, and the calico cat felt like the bear's explanation was spackle over a hole that Rheun had left in her head.

When Mazel had accepted the Rheun chip after Darius' death, she had been given a choice. She hadn't been forced to take the chip. But she also hadn't fully understood how much Rheun's presence in—and blending with—her mind would affect her. Now she knew. But in some ways, it felt too late to change her mind.

Would she go through the rest of her life feeling like she'd forgotten something? Or would the feeling fade?

It would fade.

It would have to fade. Right?

Grawf didn't prepare the meal with the synthesizer. Instead, she pulled a honeycomb out from a beehive in the corner of her quarters that was approximately the same size and shape as her with clear outer walls through which Mazel could see the bees working and buzzing busily.

Grawf claimed that O'Neill had helped her set up a pipe running from her pet beehive to the station's arboretum—a new installation that Unari had begun.

Grawf fried the piece of honeycomb up with several paws' full of wriggling white grubs from a terrarium in her quarters' other corner. Apparently, the bear was an amateur entomologist in her spare time and kept a lot of insects in her quarters.

At first, Mazel was worried that Grawf would expect her to eat the grubs while they were still alive and wriggling. Mazel wasn't interested in eating wriggling food. But once the pale white grubs were fried with honeycomb, they were quite delicious—a little crunchy on the outside with a very sweet sauce, and once she bit through them, the grubs' insides melted onto her tongue with a rich, buttery flavor.

After dinner, Grawf told Mazel stories about her time as an officer on the starship *Initiative* and eventually worked her way back to her childhood on Ursa Minuet and her people's mythology. The bear grew quite expressive, gesturing with her broad paws, as she told the wide-eyed calico cat about a beehive god who went unhinged when its queen died and a honey golem who battled with bears, testing them to see if they were worthy to enter the afterlife.

Mazel felt sure that she already knew these stories—not of Grawf's life, but of her peoples' mythology—as Rheun. But she enjoyed hearing them afresh. Even if she might remember them all for herself in the morning.

The more time she spent with Grawf, the less pressured she felt to take Rheun back. Grawf didn't care if Mazel was Mazel Tabbith or Mazel Rheun. The bear just seemed to enjoy having the little calico cat listen to her. And whenever Mazel made a joke, Grawf's laughter was deep, booming, and from the belly. Mazel loved seeing the bear laugh. It made her feel powerful to affect such a large creature so strongly.

And when Mazel didn't feel pressured to become Mazel Rheun, she had space to miss the length and depth that the ancient neural chip had brought to her life. She remembered feeling confident, powerful, and like she would live forever. Her life had been bigger when she was Mazel Rheun, and she wanted that feeling back again. She wanted her Rheun memories back.

She wanted to be Mazel Rheun.

Grawf and Mazel stayed up late into the night with the bear teaching the small calico cat various martial arts moves. Most of the moves involved imagining bees flying around her and landing in different places where she was supposed to swat at them. Mazel wasn't at all sure that swatting at bees seemed like a good idea, but since they were imaginary, she played along.

Mazel was surprised to discover that—since many of the moves involved using one's opponent's strength and weight against them—by the end of the lessons, she could regularly throw the giant bear to the floor.

Every time she did, the calico cat found herself purring. She couldn't contain the purrs. They were too big for her body and overflowed.

Eventually, Grawf surrendered: "The student has surpassed the master... if not in skill," she said, "then at least in enthusiasm." The bear folded her giant paws behind her head and stayed on the floor.

"Aren't you going to get up?" Mazel asked, itching to throw the bear on the floor again.

"No," Grawf said, eyes closed. She started humming, a tuneless rambling hum that seemed to harmonize with her colony of bees in the corner.

Mazel grabbed one of Grawf's hind paws and tried to pull her back up, but instead she ended up tumbled on the floor beside her. Grawf rolled onto her side, and crushed the little calico in place with a giant arm. "Ooh, you buzz like my bees," the bear said.

"It's called purring," Mazel objected, struggling against the giant, bushy-furred arm. But she had to admit, the bear's arm made a nice blanket. She felt safe and anchored underneath the steady weight.

Bear and cat fell asleep on the floor, cuddled together.

CHAPTER 12
RESOLVED

n the morning, Grawf walked with Mazel to the medical bay, by way of Scharm's Bar where they each had a bracing mug of hot jumaria nectar. Once Mazel felt good and jittery from the jumaria nectar, she figured she was ready to face Doctor Jardine—who probably didn't need jumaria nectar to feel energetic.

When Mazel hesitated outside the doors of the medical bay, Grawf put a giant paw on the small cat's shoulder. She didn't say anything. They hadn't talked about Mazel's fear, uncertainty, and general quandary since their brief conversation aboard *Star-Skipper 1* the night before. Sometimes, it helps more to spend time with someone and not talk about your problems. Just take a break from them.

Grawf didn't need to say that she'd still see Mazel the same way, regardless of whether the calico went into the medical bay and let Doctor Jardine return the chip to her head.

Grawf didn't know Mazel well enough yet to know the difference between Mazel Tabbith and Mazel Rheun. The differences weren't obvious on the surface. They ran deep.

Grawf lifted her paw from Mazel's shoulder and moved to leave.

"Wait," Mazel said. Maybe she didn't need to hear it—but she wanted to. "What if..."

"I don't care what you choose to do," Grawf rumbled. "But I'd like it if we could train together again. You gave me quite a workout, Little Cat."

Mazel smiled, a warm and complete smile that lifted her whiskers, twinkled in her eyes, and made her ears stand up tall. She leaned forward, pointing her pink nose upward, and the bear leaned down until her large black nose gently bumped against Mazel's small pink one. Grawf's nose was leathery and dry. And nearly as big as one of Mazel's paws. Her breath was warm and tickly in Mazel's whiskers, and it smelled of fresh loam in a rainy forest. The little cat started purring again.

"Consider it date," Mazel said. She watched the bear walk away, and then she was alone in the corridor.

She could leave, go back to her jerry-rigged, ramshackle laboratory, and simply study the data they'd collected on Nexus Nine. She could put off the decision until later.

But she didn't. She went inside, and the doctor rushed up to her, bright-eyed, bushy-tailed, and chittering a mile a minute. He wanted to hear everything about their mission through the nexus—apparently, Omoleura was still in zir chrysalis, and Neera had been tight-beaked as she kept a vigil steadfastly by the insect's side. So, Doctor Jardine had heard next to nothing about the trip, although he had removed the Rheun chip from Omoleura.

"It was the only way to make the poor fellow stop seizing," Jardine said as he scanned Mazel for the fifth time. "But you seem perfectly healthy, and we know that the Rheun chip agrees with your physiology!"

"Is that what happened?" Mazel asked, accepting a paper gown that the squirrel handed her. "The Rheun chip didn't agree with Omoleura's physiology?" She was a little worried that turning off the firewall had caused the insect's seizures.

"Most certainly," Jardine said, stepping behind a partition while Mazel changed carefully into the paper gown.

It was always challenging to not shred the delicate medical garments with her sharp claws, but she kept them carefully sheathed, in spite of the nerves that kept threatening to fluff out her fur, swish her tail, and extend the razor sharp crescents.

Jardine added, "I'm amazed that Omoleura and the Rheun chip functioned together successfully for that long. Zir brain isn't at all compatible with it! Really, it's a miracle that zhe didn't go into seizures as soon as the chip was inserted. I suppose it's a testament to the fellow's physical adaptability."

"Zhe made a true sacrifice then, in order to save the chip for me" Mazel said, tying the gown carefully around herself. "Can... I see it? Before you put it back in?"

Mazel had never actually seen the chip that had become part of her brain before—it had been removed from Darius' brain and put directly into hers while she'd been unconscious on a medical bed.

Doctor Jardine brought a shallow metal bowl to Mazel, carefully cradled in his delicate and perfectly manicured paws. In the middle of the bowl, she saw a lump of translucent jelly, approximately the size of a single one of her paw pads. Filaments of braided wires—silver, gold, and copper—extended from the jelly, looking a little like tentacles.

"It's so small," she said.

"It has to be small," Jardine replied, cradling the shallow bowl closer to his narrow chest, as if he were protecting it from her criticism. "It goes in your *brain*. There's not a lot of wasted space in brains."

"I just mean... there's so much stored in there." Mazel lowered her nose, right to the edge of the bowl and sniffed.

She smelled copper and fish oil. "It's hard to believe. That's all."

Jardine smiled and his dark eyes twinkled. His bushy tailed flipped behind him. "Are you ready to be rejoined then?"

Mazel took a deep breath and said, "Yes, please."

Doctor Jardine had Mazel lie down on the medical bed. Several rows of scanning panels rose out of the sides of the bed and rotated around until she was enclosed under their bands of flashing lights and display screens that seemed to already be showing images of the inside of her body.

Several Avioran nurses joined the squirrel doctor, and then he asked the calico cat to begin counting backwards from one hundred. She didn't feel like doing what she was told, so instead she tried to remember the words to a prayer Grawf had recited for her last night. It was a prayer that Ursine cubs made to the honey golem, asking for strength and fortitude... but Mazel only remembered the first few words.

"Grant me the fluidity, the flexibility, the ability to..."

That was all she knew.

But then the rest came to her.

"...flow like honey. Grant me the amber glow of happiness that sweet honey brings." Her voice felt creaky and small, like she hadn't used it in a long time, or maybe like it was supposed to vibrate through her whole body, instead of staying contained in a single point in her throat.

Another voice, deep and resonant, finished the prayer for Mazel: "And grant me the sticky, stucky, gummy, gluey resolve of honey in my enemy's fur." The voice laughed. "You always did love that Ursine prayer, Big Dog."

Mazel opened her eyes and saw Shep's wolfish face above her, smiling down, much like in the vision she'd had in the nexus.

Remembering the image of herself as a kitten, staring into a present filled with a river, suddenly called back a lot more memories. It almost felt like the river inside the present had flowed out to surround her, bathing her tentacles in cool, cool water. Except the water was memories. Or maybe spacetime.

Mazel closed her eyes, concentrating, trying to conjure the memories into her conscious mind, much like trying to remember a dream. But all she could recall of Omoleura's vision from the nexus that sent zim into a seizure was fragmentary snatches.

What she did remember, though, was vibrating zir wings to talk, bending zir many-jointed legs, and seeing the world through multi-faceted eyes. She remembered spitting chrysalis silk all over zirself, and she remembered the feeling of zir organs melting, reforming, and remaking zir body as she half-slept in a meditative trance.

She remembered being Omoleura.

And she remembered, during zir trance, that Shep had come to zir in a vision. Instead of telling zir, "You have a choice," as the vision of Shep had told Mazel, this vision of Shep had said something different, something more.

The words came back to her: "You have lived a long life. If the young one chooses you, live on. If the young one leaves you behind... We will have your memories here."

During the vision, Rheun had responded, speaking with a dog's mouth, a Chrysaloid's vibrating wings, and an octopus's signing tentacles. "In the nexus? You will store my memories in the nexus?"

"We live in the nexus; we built the nexus." The words were strange and incongruous coming from the German Shepherd's mouth. "We transcended our physical, tentacled bodies long ago, and even the constraints of linear time. When you returned to us, we recognized you as our own. We selected the Apex from your past and future as the individual that you were most likely to listen to—the only being who could free your host from her burden. As we speak to you in this vision, we speak to her in another one: giving her the choice."

Shep's German Shepherd body came apart in strips that waved and roiled, becoming a sea of translucent tentacles. "We have downloaded your memories, copied them, so you cannot truly die. But you also cannot live unless the small cat chooses you."

"She will choose me," the bizarre chimera-self of Rheun had said. "She will choose me."

But Rheun had not been sure.

And Mazel felt a wave of relief and gratitude roll over herself, washing her in the warmth of contentment. She had made the right choice—she was Mazel Rheun.

She was whole again.

The German Shepherd laid a gentle paw on the small cat's forehead, as if checking her temperature. "Are you all right, Big Dog?" Shep asked.

"I'm better than I've been in a long time," Mazel said. Her life was bigger and more full than it had ever been as a solitary kitten, so young that she'd only lived part of a single life, and she no longer felt driven by an inexorable force to seek an origin that had faded from her memories lifetimes ago. She had computer banks' worth of data about the nexus to study, and she had a life to live here on Nexus Nine Base.

She planned to play Chanster's Claws with Quincy and Doctor Jardine; she wanted to deepen her friendship with Neera and thank Omoleura; and she intended to best Grawf in any martial art the bear would teach her. And she would help Shep navigate the difficult waters of guiding a people who believed he had divine providence on his side—even if that divine providence was nothing more than an ancient, arcane race of octopuses living inside a space-time tunnel. She had a life to live here. And no matter how many lives she'd lived before, and no matter how many would come later, for now, she was going to focus on living this one. To its fullest.

ABOUT THE AUTHOR

Mary E. Lowd is a prolific science-fiction and furry writer in Oregon. She's had more than 200 short stories and a dozen novels published, always with more on the way. Her work has won three Ursa Major Awards, ten Leo Literary Awards, and four Cóyotl Awards. She edited FurPlanet's ROAR anthology series for five years, and she is now the editor and founder of the furry e-zine *Zooscape*. She lives in a crashed spaceship, disguised as a house and hidden behind a rose garden, with an extensive menagerie of animals, some real and some imaginary.

For more information:
marylowd.com

To read Mary's short stories:
deepskyanchor.com

ALSO BY MARY E. LOWD

Otters In Space

Otters In Space

Otters In Space 2: Jupiter, Deadly

Otters In Space 3: Octopus Ascending

Otters In Space 4: First Moustronaut

Otters In Space Spinoffs

In a Dog's World

When A Cat Loves A Dog

Jove Deadly's Lunar Detective Agency

The Entangled Universe

Entanglement Bound

The Entropy Fountain

Starwhal in Flight

Entangled Universe Spinoffs

You're Cordially Invited to Crossroads Station

Welcome to Wespirtech

Beyond Wespirtech

Xeno-Spectre

Hell Moon

The Ancient Egg

The Celestial Fragments (A Labyrinth of Souls Trilogy)

The Snake's Song

The Bee's Waltz

The Otter's Wings

Tri-Galactic Trek

Nexus Nine

Commander Annie and Other Adventures

The Necromouser and Other Magical Cats

Queen Hazel and Beloved Beverly

Some Words Burn Brightly: An Illuminated Collection of Poetry

www.ingramcontent.com/pod-product-compliance
Lightning Source LLC
Chambersburg PA
CBHW031623170726
47990CB00016B/347